THE TIME WATCHERS

A Tale of Sleepover Terror

Robbie Myles

**THIS BOOK IS FOR
JUDY, ERIC, MAXI, ZENDA AND KANTER.**

Copyright © 2022 by Robbie Myles

Cover Art Copyright © 2022 by Art to Zombies, LLC.

All rights reserved, including the right to reproduce this book or portions thereof in any form whatsoever.

This book is a work of fiction. Any references to historical events, real people, or real places are used fictitiously. Other names, characters, places and events are products of the author's imagination, and any resemblance to actual events or places or persons, living or dead, is entirely coincidental.

Forward

I've been under the spell of scary stories for as long as I've known how to read, but my obsession with horror books began long before that. As a toddler, I would find myself wandering among the stacks of my local library, eagerly seeking out the latest book in the *Goosebumps* series by R.L. Stine or the newest ghost story from Betty Ren Wright. I didn't know how to read these books for myself at the time, no—but there was something about the crackling of the binding that mesmerized me, made me think of dry bones clawing their way out of a rickety casket. Then there were the ghostly words floating from my mother's lips as she recited these eerie tales to me before bed. It was this early planting of the seed that instilled a lifelong love of spooky stories deep inside me, a seed that has branched off into me writing spooky stories of my own.

One of my favorite parts of being a horror author is interacting with other writers who share my taste for the eerie and the weird, especially those who derive inspiration from those same children's horrors I mentioned previously. Robbie Myles is one of those authors.

When Robbie's previous novel *Don't Call at ALL* graced my sights, I was transported back to my youth—just a nerdy boy scavenging the library shelves, searching for terrifying tales to scratch my itch for horror and finding just what I needed in Robbie's familiar, nostalgic voice.

Fast forward just a short year later and we have a new tale from Robbie Myles—*The Time Watchers*, the first book in a new series that is sure to bewitch children both young and old. Folks of my generation will likely pick up on notes of *Hocus Pocus*, *Ernest Scared Stupid*, *Goosebumps*, *Killer Klowns from Outer Space,* and fantasy films of yesteryear, while children of today may be reminded of adventure stories by Brandon Mull and Rick Riordan.

Either way, this Halloween extravaganza delivers the goopy-gory goods with a plethora of monsters and beasties of all varieties, everything from insect-munching witches to giant jelly monsters, a terrifying trio of trick-or-treaters, undead skeletons, and a larger-than-life villain that is equal parts intimidating and campy.

Monsters aside, however, *The Time Watchers* is a story of friendship first-and-foremost, of working together in the face of evil and stopping at nothing to rescue the ones you love. Afterall, there is a super epic Halloween sleepover to get back to, and the snacks aren't going to eat themselves!

I hope you, reader, enjoy this creepy Halloween romp as much as I did. Trick-or-treat!

- Cameron Chaney, 2021

"Many adults feel that every children's book has to teach them something . . .
My theory is a children's book . . .
can be just for fun."

-R.L. STINE

1

Heavy gusts of wind blew through a long, dark, wet, and cold cavern. Bugs, worms, and other creepy-crawlies made their way along its walls. The cavern's path followed deep down, into parts unknown.

Eventually, a long hall of the cave opened up to a large clearing where "the Watcher" sat on his throne of clocks, waiting in silence. The Watcher watched as the clocks surrounding him everywhere ticked and tocked.

There were clocks in heaping piles lining the floor and clocks lining the cavern's walls. Everywhere that could be seen was surrounded by clocks of all shapes and sizes. Some were small and short, while others stood large, as tall as a giraffe. One particular clock that hung from the ceiling of the Watcher's lair was black all over, and it seemed to be breathing in and out. It had pointed spikes on all sides. Each of the clocks in the Watcher's cave ticked to a different time.

A wretched hag, draped in a black cloak, limped along as she approached the Watcher. "Master, master!"

she hissed. "I've brought you a treat. Look for yourself, feast your eyes on this disgusting, filthy little boy!"

The Watcher looked on as the hag dragged a young boy by his heels behind her.

The hag's veiny, decrepit hand pulled the boy across the dirt of the cavern and laid him at the foot of the throne of clocks.

At first, the Watcher didn't pay her any mind. He just stared coldly into the clocks surrounding him.

"Can I keep him, master? Oh please, can I make him mine? And bring him down into the dungeons, to be with me forever?"

"SILENCE!" The Watcher still kept his gaze on the clocks, not looking at Gramilda the witch. The Watcher's voice was a blast through the entire cavern.

Clocks clinked and clanked as they fell from the walls to the ground.

The Watcher stood up from his throne of clocks. His enormous body cast a shadow over Gramilda and the boy. He took several steps off his throne. Gramilda nervously backed away.

The boy's eyes opened with terror as the Watcher grabbed him by his shirt collar and lifted him high into the air.

The Watcher palmed the boy in just one hand. Slowly, the Watcher began sucking in deep breaths, each exhausting the boy more. Seemingly stealing away his energy, his life force. The boy's skin turned a milkier white with each breath taken.

The Watcher took in one final breath of the boy's

inner essence, then dropped his lifeless body onto the sea of clocks.

The boy lay there motionless. In his heart and mind, he knew he was still alive. But in his soul, he knew there was something missing. He had no happy thoughts. Now, he was consumed by only darkness.

"Go now, Gramilda. Take him down into the dungeon, make him a slave. Make him our slave . . . forever!"

The witch jumped up in excitement while the cavern rattled from the Watcher's words. A large green vein pulsed in Gramilda's hand as she grabbed the boy's ankle and raced away, down the long corridor. The frumpy, tattered witch's evil laugh echoed off the clocks that surrounded her everywhere but not before she tripped on her own left foot. Clumsy one, Gramilda was.

The Watcher looked on in disgust. "Oh, Gramilda. You fool."

"I'm all right, master!" Gramilda screeched back from down the deep corridor. "I'm just DANDYYYYYY!" Gramilda's words echoed through the entire underground lair as she continued scurrying away.

In the main chamber of the Watcher's cave, thousands of milky, pale, soulless children stood locked in a trance. Working for the Watcher, they grinded the many levers and switches needed to power his clock tower. They were unfazed by the noise. One boy seemed to momentarily stop winding a rather large handle attached to what seemed to be a windmill, but he continued on merely seconds later.

The Watcher, the evilest being that ever existed, looked around his main chamber. His clocks continued to click and tick. One particular clock caught his eye, though. He stood tall, a behemoth, a sight to behold, and walked over to it. The clock seemed to be glowing. The clock radiated its force into the Watcher.

"Yes," he said. "I'll be there soon, little one. Sooner than you can imagine." And with his words, the Watcher let out a giant laugh. A sound so sinister and vile. His next target had been chosen.

2

"Hey, that's my cheese!" Emmy said. "Give it back, doofus!" Emmy stared in disbelief, as Sam was slurping on a rather large piece of cheese that had fallen off of her slice of pizza.

"Sorry, Emmy," Sam said. "It came off with my piece, so it's my cheese." Although the cheese was burning the roof of his mouth, Sam was smiling ear to ear.

"Mrs. Strong, Sam stole all the cheese off my slice!" Emmy cried out.

Mrs. Strong, Sam's mom, walked over to the table where the three best friends Emmy, Sam and Jack were sitting. She couldn't help but laugh.

Emmy's slice of pizza looked more like roadkill than food. Half of her slice was missing.

"I'll tell you what, hunnie, give me this, and you go ahead and take another piece, okay?"

Before she handed the mangled slice to Mrs. Strong, Emmy pretended to launch it over at Sam.

"Hey, watch it!" Sam said. "I'm wearing my lucky shirt!" Sam always wore his green shamrock shirt on sleepover nights. It was his favorite.

Emmy handed Mrs. Strong the slice, or what was left of it, and grabbed another piece. She took one bite and grimaced at Sam, showing her displeasure for what he had done.

"Hey, Emmy, what's that?" Jack pointed to the hallway.

Emmy looked over to where Jack was pointing before realizing she was being fooled.

"Gotcha!" Jack ripped a piece of cheese off of the brand-new slice Emmy had just taken from the box.

"Mrs. Strong!" Emmy complained. She got up and moved two seats down from both boys. Although they were her best friends, she was not happy. She sat and huffed.

Emmy, Jack, and Sam had always been best friends. They had grown up in the same neighborhood since the start of first grade, all of their parents were friends and they hung out every day.

They also loved sleepovers. Although they often switched up the house they stayed at, Sam's was their preference because his room was in the basement. In his room, they could stay up all night, talk, play games, and look at videos on the internet.

But this particular sleepover was special because it was for a whole weekend! It was also Halloween, which fell on a Saturday this year. It had all the makings of the best weekend of all time.

The plan was to hang out Friday night, watch scary movies, tell stories, and then wake up Saturday for a full day of fun Halloween activities. Last year, Sam's mom helped them carve their first jack-o'-lanterns! Emmy's didn't turn out so well, and the boys never wasted an opportunity to remind her.

The three best friends finished their pizza, guzzled down some soda, and made their way down into Sam's room for movie night.

"Do you three have everything you need?" Mrs. Strong was patting down and fluffing Sam's pillow as she spoke.

"Yes, we are all good, Mom. Love you," Sam said.

"Your father needs his sleep, so keep the noise down. I expect you troublemakers to be in bed and sleeping by ten! Nothing good happens when you stay up late," Mrs. Strong said. "Especially not on Devil's Night." She stared coldly at Sam, Emmy, and Jack.

"Mrs. Strong, I've got this covered," Emmy spoke. "I'll make sure these two head to bed at a reasonable hour. You have nothing to worry about."

"Well, all right then, I believe you." Mrs. Strong had a smile on her face that said, *I don't actually believe you.* She kissed all three of the kids good night and walked back upstairs. She reached the door at the top of the step and looked back down at Sam, Emmy, and Jack. "Please don't make me come back down here." She closed the door behind her.

"That was funny, don't you think?" Sam said.

"She actually thinks we'll go to bed early!" Jack

laughed. "The whole point of a sleepover is to stay up late. Everybody knows that. *Especially* on Devil's Night."

"You guys are the worst," Emmy plopped down to the floor.

"Okay, so back to our task at hand. What are we going to watch?" Sam shifted his attention to the television screen.

"Can we please not watch something scary?" Emmy cried out.

"Not watch something scary? But it's Devil's Night, the night before Halloween. We have to!" Jack always loved scary movies.

Sam picked up the remote and clicked on the TV. "Okay, let's see what we've got here." Sam scrolled through the movie channels.

"These movies stink," Emmy said. Her sleeping bag was wrapped around her head like a tortilla.

"Yeah, I've seen all of these," Jack said.

"Okay. Well, how about this, then?" Sam shut off the TV, dimmed the lights, and sat on the floor next to his friends. "Have you guys ever heard of . . . the Watcher?"

Emmy and Jack both looked at each other, then back at Sam.

"The Watcher?" Emmy said.

"What, did he stutter?" Jack clapped back at Emmy.

"Quiet, you two," Sam said. "Yes, the Watcher."

Emmy knew from Sam's tone this was going to be something spooky.

"The legend of the Watcher has been told and

passed down many generations," Sam said.

"Is this the one about the guy in the mirror that gets you when you say his name five times?" Emmy said.

"Of course not, dingus. It's the one about—" Jack was trying to speak before Sam cut him off.

"Shh! Quiet! You're going to wake up my parents." Sam did his best to keep his voice low and get the point across. He picked up his cell phone, put on the flashlight and held it under his neck to light up his face. "The Watcher is the evilest being that ever lived." Emmy and Jack listened intently. "Nobody really knows where he's from or where he lives. But somewhere underneath the ground, the Watcher lurks. He sits on his throne of clocks and watches all the children in the world."

"What do you mean, he watches them?" Emmy said.

"He *only* feeds on children," Sam said. "Sucks the life force from them. Turns them into slaves to work in his dungeon and power up his clocks."

"Did you say clocks?" Jack chimed in.

"Yes, clocks," Sam answered. "The Watcher keeps a clock for every kid in the entire world. He watches us all, at all times. He watches us when we eat and when we're at school. He watches us at camp, at the dinner table, or playing video games. He even watches us in our sleep. He always watches."

Emmy wrapped her sleeping bag tighter around her body. "I don't think I like this story," she said.

"No kid has ever escaped the clutches of the Watcher," Sam grimaced. "Once he gets you down into his underground lair of levers and buttons and clocks, it's over."

"It's . . . over?" Emmy said.

"It's *over!*" Sam responded.

There was a brief moment of silence before Jack spoke out. "Nah, I don't believe it. The Watcher's not real."

"Is, too!" Emmy said.

"Of course he's real," Sam stated his case. "The Watcher is as real as you and me." He gave a long pause before continuing. "Just because we can't see him doesn't mean he isn't under the ground, right here in Mill Falls."

"What was that?" Jack said. "Did you guys just hear that?"

"Hear what?" Emmy's eyes wandered.

Jack looked around the room. "You didn't hear that? It can't be."

"No! Tell me, what is it!?" Emmy said.

Jack stood and put his ear against the bedroom wall. "I think it's coming from here. No, no, wait. I think it's coming from over here." Jack ran over to the desk and put his ear up to it. Jack waltzed around the room and checked several other spots before locking his eyes onto Emmy.

"What? What is it? Why are you staring at me!?" Emmy said.

"Tick, tock, tick, tock," Jack said. "Can't you guys hear it? I thought it was coming from the wall, and then

I thought it was over by the desk. But now, I think it's coming from right where you're sitting, Emmy."

Emmy shot up and dropped her sleeping bag to the floor. "It can't be, Jack. It can't be!"

Jack slowly strolled over to the spot where Emmy had been sitting. Hesitantly, he began to lower his ear to the ground. "Yes, I think this is it. It's coming from right here. I can just barely make it out. Tick, tock. Tick, tock. Tick, tock."

Just as Jack's ear was pressed directly down to the ground, Emmy let out a loud shriek, as something grabbed her from behind.

"AHHHHHHHHH!" Emmy screamed for her life.

3

Emmy jerked forward and free from the hands that grabbed her. Then she turned around and heard the laughs. Sam, giggling like a hyena, was standing there.

"You should have seen your face!" Sam said.

"I totally got it on my phone!" Jack said as he scrolled through his phone to pull up the video.

"UGH! Give me that, now!" Emmy walked up to Jack and tried to grab the phone from his hand. The two continued wrestling for Jack's phone when the light from the staircase turned on.

"What is going on down here?" Mrs. Strong said, thumping down the staircase. Sam, Jack, and Emmy all turned in terror, their faces ghostly white with embarrassment. Jack's phone fell to the floor.

"Nothing, Mom! Just getting ready for bed," Emmy and Jack were silent.

"Getting ready for bed? I heard a scream! Is everything all right down here?"

"Yeah, Mom. Thanks for checking in, we're fine."

"All right, then. Keep it down, you three. I don't want to come down here again. Your father is trying to sleep, Samuel," Mrs. Strong said. "Remember what I said about going to bed early. Nothing good comes from staying up late. Especially not tonight!"

"I gotcha, no problem, Mom. We're sorry, we're going to bed now, all right, good night." Sam pushed his mom back up the stairs and out of the basement.

"I knew you were going to wake up my mom!" Sam said.

"Hey, this was all your fault, bozos! I didn't ask you to scare me like that," Emmy said.

"Jack, did you actually get the video?" Sam had a big smile on his face.

"I sure did!" Jack picked up his phone from the floor and scrolled to his videos. "It's gone! I must have accidentally deleted it when I dropped it."

"Great," Sam said. "All that for nothing. Thanks a lot, Emmy."

Emmy looked at Sam. A slow smile spread across her face. She couldn't help but laugh. Although Jack and Sam were always playing and messing around with her, deep down she knew that they only did it because they cared about her. The trio had been friends for so long that she was used to it. She also kind of liked the attention they always gave her. "You better be careful, Sammy!" Emmy said. "The Watcher doesn't like little boys who play tricks on their friends!" Emmy grabbed hold of Sam and tickled him down to the ground.

The trio messed around for another half hour or so

before calling it a night. All was well in the Strong household. Sam lay comfortably in his bed, fast asleep. His two best friends, Jack and Emmy, were right next to him on the floor, wrapped in their sleeping bags. If only they knew their lives were about to change forever.

Sam was having the most excellent dream before the eerie voice had woken him up.

In his dream, it was Halloween. Sam, Emmy, and Jack had just returned to Sam's house from a long night of trick-or-treating. They sat down in Sam's room, all three on the floor, enjoying their candy.

"Oh man, look at this haul!" Jack said. "It's like a never-ending supply, check it out!" Jack dumped his pillowcase out onto the floor of Sam's room. The candy kept coming out. The three had to back up just for it all to fit.

"You think that's a nice haul? Check out this!" Emmy followed suit and dumped all of her candy onto the pile.

"Oh please, that's nothing. You both know I got the best haul, and it's not even close." Sam dumped his candy out onto the pile, which was now a massive mountain of chocolates, candies, lollipops, and licorice. A rainbow mountain of deliciousness.

Quickly, they began unwrapping goodies left and right. Candy after candy, they went on stuffing their mouths and laughing. Sam had eyed one particular bite-size chocolate bar, unwrapped it, threw it up into the air, and back down into his mouth. That was when he heard the voice. *"Samuel."* It called out his name. He looked over to the staircase where it came from . . .

Sam woke up, startled. *Just a dream*, he thought. He rubbed his eyes on his shirt and lay back down, his pillow a fluffy marshmallow of comfort.

"Samuel," the voice called out again.

Sam jerked up in his bed. This time, he was not dreaming. He looked down at Jack and Emmy, who were sleeping, and then back up to the staircase it was coming from. "Mom?" Sam whispered, doing his best not to wake his friends. "Mom, is that you?"

Sam quietly pulled the blanket off of his body, got out of bed, tiptoeing to not wake up Emmy or Jack. He inched around them both and their sleeping bags, to the edge of the staircase.

"Mom? Is everything okay?" Sam said.

"Samuel, can you help me? Come quickly!" the voice said.

The voice was still little more than a whisper, so it was hard for Sam to really make out who was talking. His first thought would have been that Emmy and Jack were just messing around with him, but their snores relieved that. Sam took one more look at his sleeping friends, then started heading up the staircase toward the voice that called to him.

"Is everything all right? Mom? Dad?" Sam said as he reached the top of the staircase, but neither of his parents replied.

Sam walked through the kitchen, creeping along the floor, looking for the voice, the thing that called to him. *"I'm over here, Samuel! I need your help. Please, come help me!"* the voice said.

Sam inspected the area where the voice came from and saw nothing. There was no one there. He walked over to the sliding porch door and opened it. *"That's it, Sam. You're much closer now. I'm right over here!"* Now the voice was much louder.

Sam continued on out toward the bushes in his backyard. He knew now that the voice was just beyond this area. The cold, dewy grass crunched underneath his feet as he walked, step-by-step. A cold chill overcame him. He rubbed his arms for warmth.

"Is everything all right, ma'am? Sir?" Sam said.

"Just a little bit closer now, Samuel. Just a few more steps, and I can show you, my sweet, delicious little boy," the voice beckoned.

A thought washed over Sam's mind: *What am I doing? Why am I outside in the middle of the night?* But the voice calling to him kept his attention transfixed. Sam wanted to turn away and go back to his fluffy bed, in his comfortable room, right next to his best friends. But something in the voice kept him locked in. He couldn't walk away.

Sam took one more step toward the bush when a disgusting, green, veiny hand shot out and grabbed him by the shirt collar. He jerked back immediately, and his shirt ripped! He made one dash to run away and scream for help, but before he could even react in time, the other hand shot out and grabbed him, clutching with incredible force. The gross hands pulled him through the bush and into a clearing. He was staring face-to-face with an old, wrinkled, green-skinned witch!

"Good evening, Samuel," Gramilda the witch said, her voice now an eerie, raspy sound. "The Watcher will see you now." And Gramilda cackled on as she carried Sam off into the night.

4

Emmy and Jack woke up to a faint ray of light that shone in through Sam's window. "Hey, wake up, doofus." Jack threw a pillow at Emmy.

"I am up, dingus," Emmy said groggily. "Throw another pillow, I dare you." Emmy sat up, her long, cherry blonde hair a disaster. She looked over at Jack through half-shut eyes. "He up yet?" she said, pointing at Sam's bed.

"Don't think so. I guess there's only one way to find out, don't you agree?" Jack said as he lifted his other pillow and stood up and out of his sleeping bag.

Emmy followed and did the same. The two walked over to Sam's bed in preparation.

"On my count of three," Jack said. "One . . ." Jack whispered. "Two . . ." Another whisper. "THREE!" Jack roared. And on his third count, Emmy and Jack both launched their pillows onto Sam's bed. They came down thunderously with their pillows several times before realizing he wasn't there.

"That's weird," Emmy said. "He must have gone up for breakfast."

Jack said nothing but took a long, hard look at Emmy. He stared her up and down, pillow in hand. Emmy realized before it was too late, and Jack initiated a rainstorm of pillow hits across her.

"Let's go find him," Jack said, breathing heavily from the pillow fight.

"I think I'm going to have a mark, you dingus."

"That will teach you not to pick a pillow fight with me next time."

"I didn't pick anything! You started it!" Emmy cried out.

Reaching the top of the staircase and heading into the kitchen, Emmy and Jack looked around. Everything was frozen in stillness. Light shined in through the curtained shades on the sliding-glass window. Two coffee mugs were in the sink. A note had been left on the counter:

Bagels on the table. Cream cheese and butter in the fridge! Dad and I went for a walk. No fighting! I know exactly how many pumpkin cookies are in the jar. Happy Halloween!

Emmy looked over at the oven clock. 9:34 a.m. "Well, at least we know where the rest of the Strongs are," she said. Emmy took a plate from the counter, pulled out the cream cheese from the fridge, and brought it over to the table. "Breakfast time."

"What are you doing?" Jack said.

"What does it look like I'm doing?" Emmy responded. "I'm about to have myself a nice breakfast, courtesy of Mr. and Mrs. Strong."

"Where is Sam?" Jack asked.

"How should I know?" Emmy spread the cream cheese on her bagel as she spoke.

"Don't you think we should look for him?"

"Look for him? Dude, he's probably upstairs showering, or in the backyard. Chill out," Emmy said. "SAMMY!!" Emmy called out through a mouthful of everything bagel and cream cheese, obviously not concerned at the moment with where her friend was.

Jack called out, too. "Sam? You upstairs?" There was no response.

Jack opened the sliding-glass door behind Emmy and walked onto the backyard patio. "Hey, Sam! You out here?!" Jack called out. Again, there was no response.

Jack walked around the patio and surveyed the area. *This isn't like Sam*, he thought to himself. *Where could he be?* Jack was about to walk back inside when he noticed something in the grass, just beyond the patio. A mark, a spot that sat differently than the rest of the backyard. *A footprint?*

Slowly and cautiously, Jack walked down the patio steps and out into the backyard. "Hey, dingus, what are you doing out there?" Emmy called out to him.

Jack did not respond. His attention was laser focused. Something didn't feel right.

Jack made it over to the odd spot on the grass and bent down on one knee. *It is a footprint*, he thought. Jack looked ahead. The glare of the morning sun was doing a good job of blinding his sight from what was ahead. He took a few steps forward, and low and behold, another footprint.

Although it was unmistakably a footprint, Jack was having a hard time believing it to be Sam's. It wasn't your standard sneaker-bottom shoe print. This was something different. The footprint Jack was staring down at must have been from an animal. It was humongous. This thing's foot had to be double the size of Sam's. No way this was Sam's footprint. It also seemed to split in half, almost into two different feet. It was separated into two diagonal sections, forming the shape of a V.

Jack kept walking and found another footprint and another. The prints kept going and led him into the bush on the side of Sam's house.

Jack walked slowly back through the brisk morning air, dewy grass and up the steps of the Strong family's back porch. He carefully opened the screen door, walked back into the kitchen, and sat down quietly next to Emmy, who was scarfing down her bagel and cream cheese.

"There's a really weird footprint out there," Jack said.

"No durr, dingus face. We live in Mill Falls. There is wildlife everywhere. Remember that time the whole family of deer came into—"

Jack didn't let Emmy finish her sentence. "This isn't a deer's footprint." Jack had no idea what kind of creature would leave a print like the one he saw, but he knew for sure it wasn't any deer. Nor was it his best friend Sam's.

"Did you sleep all right, dude? Are you okay? Maybe you should eat something." Emmy put the back of her hand up to Jack's forehead to fake check his temperature.

Jack swatted Emmy's hand away. "I'm serious! Stop messing around. This footprint is huge!"

"All right, all right. Let's go." Emmy stood up with a mouth full of bagel, put on her shoes, and followed Jack out into the backyard.

Jack led Emmy down to the spot where he saw the print, but it was gone. There was nothing there. "It was right here!" Jack said. "Emmy, I swear! It was huge, and it was not normal."

"It's freezing, my feet are wet, and my bagel's getting cold for this," Emmy, clearly not happy, said.

"You have to believe me, it was right here!" Jack was confused. *The print was there just moments before, wasn't it?*

"I'm going back inside." Emmy started walking back up to the porch and into the Strong's kitchen.

"Emmy, wait." Jack took several steps toward the bushes the prints had led him to when he found them just a few minutes prior. He spread the branches and leaves of the bush slightly with both hands. Out of the corner of his eye, Jack noticed something dangling. He examined it closely and plucked it off of the branch.

"Emmy, come back here. You're not going to believe this," Jack called out to Emmy.

5

"EMMY!" Jack screamed her name this time. "Get out here, now!"

"I didn't even make it back inside yet, dingus." Emmy walked back down the stairs of the porch, over the wet grass, and back to where Jack was standing by the bush. "What is it?"

"Look. Do you recognize this?" Jack had found a small piece of cloth hanging from one of the branches on the bush. He held it up to Emmy's face.

"Looks like a dirty piece of cloth." Emmy was not amused.

"Not just a dirty piece of cloth, Emmy. A dirty piece of *Sam's shirt!*"

Emmy took the piece of cloth from Jack and examined it. It was green, and it had a small white spot in the corner. "This *is* Sam's shirt!" she said.

It was definitely a piece from Sam's lucky shirt, which he had been wearing the night before.

"Something weird is going on," Jack said.

Emmy had a nervous look on her face. She was confused. "Okay, well, there has to be some kind of reasonable explanation for this, right?"

"I don't know, Emmy. I have a bad feeling about this." Jack grabbed the piece of shirt back from Emmy and examined it.

Jack and Emmy stood for a moment in silence, in awe of the hanging threads of Sam's shirt in Jack's hand.

Jack gripped the shirt with one hand and marched forward, again toward the bush where he had found the piece of shirt.

"Where are you going?" Emmy asked.

Jack didn't respond; instead, he was walking with a purpose. No time to respond. There was something odd happening in the backyard of Samuel P. Strong, in the quaint town of Mill Falls.

Jack gazed at the thick bush for a moment before turning his attention beyond it. Jack kept walking and followed it around back to track the area behind.

"Where are you going, dingus breath?" Emmy called out to Jack.

Still, Jack did not respond. He was possessed and seemed to be on a mission.

"Helloooo?!" Emmy quickly realized Jack was not going to respond at this point. "UGH!" Emmy humphed and followed Jack, who was now out of sight behind the bush.

"THERE!" Jack yelled out, as Emmy approached from behind.

"What is it?" Emmy responded.

"Look, quickly!" Jack ran over to the large footprint in the grass and dirt behind the large bush where they had found Sam's shirt. "I knew I saw something!"

Emmy ran over to where Jack was standing. "What the heck is that thing?"

"I told you! This is the footprint I saw back in Sam's backyard. It's the same one!" Jack said.

"But what is it? I mean, what kind of animal could have made a print like this?" Emmy was shocked and confused. None of this made any sense.

Then, right before their eyes, something very weird happened.

"I suppose it could be a large coyote. I've never actually seen a coyote's print, but Mom says they are pretty big," Emmy said.

"Hey, look! What's happening to it?!"

Jack and Emmy stood, staring fixedly at the large print on the ground, but it seemed to be fading away. The print was actually disappearing right in front of them.

"Where did it go?" Emmy said.

"It's gone! It just disappeared!" Jack looked all around the grassy area behind the bush for an answer. Anything that might give them a hint, a clue. "Look!" Jack pointed over to another print just a few feet away.

Emmy and Jack ran over to the new print that they saw. "It looks exactly the same; it has to be from the same animal."

Just a few seconds after they reached it, the print they were now staring at started to fade away and disappear as well.

"This is too weird," Emmy said. "We need to keep going, there have to be more of these!"

Emmy and Jack walked on and found another print, then another. They kept walking until they were in their neighbors', the Gordons', backyard. Print by print, they began to follow the trail. Each print disappeared right in front of their eyes.

"Are we sure we want to keep following these prints?" Emmy questioned.

"This has to lead us to Sam," Jack said.

"But what if it leads us to Sam, and something else . . ."

Jack didn't really know what that meant, but the two friends stopped following the prints for a moment. They stared at each other for a minute, frozen in time.

"Whatever we find, we'll brave it together," Jack said.

"For Sam," Emmy responded, her eyes fiery globes of emotion.

They kept on trudging through the grass covering the backyards of Mill Falls. They had uncovered so many prints, and tracked so much land, that they weren't exactly sure where they had gone to.

The prints led them to a large clearing somewhere in the back woods of Mill Falls. They followed three final prints and stopped at a large, peculiar-looking tree.

"Is that it?" Emmy said.

"I don't see any other prints," Jack glanced around.

"All I see is this stupid tree. Stupid and ugly. I don't like it."

"It's just a tree," Jack said.

The tree they had arrived at didn't look like an ordinary tree. Its trunk was blacker than it was brown. The darkest, saddest tree they had ever seen. The branches were thin, long, and wiry, horrible fingers reaching out for help, but its base was massive. Thick and low to the ground. There were no leaves; it must have been dead for thousands of years. It was unlike anything they had seen in their lives.

Both Emmy and Jack circled the tree looking for more prints, anything that could help continue to lead them to a sign or symbol in the right direction. They both knew the oddness of what was happening, but they also knew that it had to be connected to Sam's disappearance.

Jack, tired and hungry, was sitting down with his back against the tree when he heard the evil, high-pitched echo of a laugh.

"What was that?" Jack stood up immediately and turned to face the tree.

"What was what?" Emmy responded.

"It came from in there."

"In the tree?" Emmy asked.

"Yes, in the tree. It was a laugh! A high-pitched *shriek* of a laugh!"

Jack had grave concern in his eyes as he looked

through the tree for an answer. Nothing came to him.

"I swear I heard a laugh come from the tree! It's like it came from *inside* the tree," Jack said.

Emmy and Sam circled the tree, looking for anything that might give them a clue. They put their ears up to its trunk and tried to listen for something, anything.

Jack and Emmy were taking a close look at the black roots of the tree when they heard the loud noise.

"Jack, watch out!" Emmy yelled.

6

A loud *POP* startled the two of them. A steady humming sound followed shortly after.

"Jack, look!" Emmy grabbed Jack's hand and pulled him behind a nearby bush.

There was something happening at the base of the tree. The humming continued, and something was opening. *A door?* Emmy and Jack were terrified and confused all at once. They were lost in the chaos unfolding in front of them.

A large, dark wooden panel was slowly rising from the base of the tree. As it did, small patches of smoke slowly crept out.

"What is happening? What is that?" Emmy said, staring in disbelief.

"It looks like some kind of door," Jack whispered back to Emmy, as quietly as possible.

Things got even weirder for Emmy and Jack as a hefty, thick creature with green, slimy skin emerged from the door and smoke clouds.

Gramilda the witch hopped along, smiling a huge, toothless grin on her way out of the blackened tree. "La da dee dum, la da dee dom," Gramilda hummed, dancing and prancing with each step.

"Oh, a delicious slug!" Gramilda bent down and picked up a large, writhing, slimy worm of a bug and held it up to her mouth. Before she had a chance to eat it, she clumsily dropped it back to the dirt floor. "Oh, drats. Come back here, I hate chasing after my food." Gramilda took two giant steps in pursuit of the slug and tripped on her own feet. Lying on her stomach, she now stared eye to eye with the little insect giving her so much trouble. She smiled and slurped it up off the ground with no hands.

"Ew, gross!" Emmy whispered to Jack.

"Shhh!" Jack couldn't take his eyes off Gramilda. He couldn't believe what he was seeing.

Gramilda, with bits of black slug remains surrounding her mouth, stood up and pranced along the grass and out of sight.

"What . . . on Earth . . . was that?" Jack said, slowly walking out from behind the bush he had been hiding in.

"Green skin, big black hat, eats bugs? I'm going to say that was a witch, Jack."

"Well, yes, I think you're right. It's definitely a witch. But how many witches have *you* seen lately, Emmy?" Jack spoke, still looking off into the distance to make sure Gramilda the witch was not in view.

Emmy and Jack were startled again when the panel

door at the base of the tree began rumbling again.

"Jack, quick!" Emmy dropped to the ground and slithered her way into the smoke-filled door that Gramilda had come out of.

Hesitantly following her lead, Jack hit the ground and shimmied his way on in to the smoky trees' darkness.

The door closed alarmingly forcefully behind them. In order to get out, if they ever were to get out, Emmy and Jack had no idea how they would do it. Although they were barely able to see, Emmy and Jack both took in deep breaths and gazed at each other.

"Where are we?" Jack said, swatting away the smoke that surrounded his face.

"I think we're in the tree," Emmy said.

"Yeah, no durr, Einstein," Jack responded.

"What a weird day. This is all so twisted," Emmy said, taking her first step down into the unknown of the tree. "Do you think Sam's in here?"

"He's got to be. Doesn't he?"

"I suppose. Let's go find him before that witch comes back through this door."

Emmy and Jack took several steps ahead, staying close by each other. Each step they took made a sucking sound, like they were walking through the thickest mud. There wasn't much light for them to see around them. All they knew, in that moment, was that they needed to find Sam. Wherever they were, whatever place this was, it was not a good one.

They moved forward together and with caution. Looking around, trying to make out anything they could in the darkness with each step.

After a few moments, they were able to see a small stream of light coming from up ahead. "Look at that!" Emmy said to Jack. "I think there's some light. Up ahead."

Jack confirmed Emmy's happy thoughts. "Yeah, let's make it there in one piece. Be careful where you step; it's all sludgy."

Emmy and Jack made it to the clearing where the light was, and what they saw all around them was startling.

"There must be a thousand passageways here!" Back-to-back, Emmy and Jack rotated the cavern in a circle. They eyed each passage down. They all looked the same.

"Well, which do we take?" Jack said.

"How am I supposed to know, dingus? Do I look like I've been here before?" Emmy said.

The good news is that this part of the cave seemed to have hard, sturdy ground. There was still no light in the cavern they came in through, but they could feel and see bits of the mushy ground on their feet.

"What are you doing?" Jack asked Emmy.

"Give me your shoelaces," Emmy demanded.

"My shoelaces? Why do you want my shoelaces?"

"Come on, let's go! Quickly, before that witch comes back!" Emmy cried out.

Jack followed orders. One by one, on each of his

shoes, he began pulling and unknotting. His shoes were soon lace free. He handed both of his laces to Emmy and watched her plan unfold.

"Stay here," Emmy said, walking back down the corridor they came from. "Don't move, I'll be right back."

"Emmy, where are you going? Don't leave me!"

Emmy ran back down the cavern they came in through, and the darkness quickly engulfed her.

Jack stood silently in the middle chamber of this large cavern of halls. He looked around at the massive pathways and caves surrounding him. It was truly an unbelievable sight, like nothing he had ever seen before or would see again. Or so he thought. Jack also realized in that moment he had never felt so alone before.

"Emmy, come quickly!" Jack realized he didn't remember which cavern they had come through and where Emmy ran back to. They all looked exactly the same! *How are we going to get out of here?* Jack thought.

Jack was on the verge of panic when Emmy emerged from the dark of the cavern. "All right, all set?" Emmy said.

Jack ran over to Emmy, put his arms around her, and hugged her. "I missed you, Emmy."

"Dude, get a grip. I was gone for, like, two seconds."

Jack smiled at her, relieved to see her face. The feelings of being alone went away instantly.

"Okay, so look," Emmy said. "I took your shoelaces, and I lined the cave wall that we came in through. You can see it poking out of the light right over there."

"Oh man! Good call, Emmy!"

"This way, we can trace our way back out of here, and we know which cavern we came out of. Got it?" Emmy said.

"Got it," Jack responded.

"Let's go find our best friend," Emmy said.

And with those words, Jack and Emmy began down one of the many paths in the dark cave they were in.

7

Sam's arms had begun tiring. Although he didn't know exactly how long he had been trapped in this underground cave of levers and switches, it felt like an eternity. He had no idea where he was. Were his friends okay? His parents? The last thing he remembered before being down there was a voice calling out to him, calling his name. He had followed it because he thought someone was in danger and needed his help.

Sam was weak and tired. He felt constantly dizzy, like he was weightless. Sam looked around and realized just how massive this structure was. He was helping to operate what looked like a gigantic wooden tree house. There were wooden poles attached to boxes that went as high up as Sam could see. Thousands of dials, levers, and switches were constantly being pushed by children just like Sam. They all looked deathly pale. Their movements were slow and mechanical.

I've got to get out of here. Sam still had his memories and small shreds of energy. Although his memories came in patches, minutes would go by where he wouldn't think a single thought. He would come to his senses randomly and again remember his friends, his family, his desire to get out of this place. The problem was that his mind would tell him one thing, but his body would barely cooperate. He had very little energy and could tell it was draining more and more by the second.

Mustering as much energy as his body would allow in that moment, Sam stopped rolling his lever. His arm lay at rest by his side. *What a relief.* Sam took several steps away from the giant tree house of levers. Step by step he walked, slowly but carefully.

One boy that stood on the second level of the tree house creaked his neck in Sam's direction. They locked eyes. For a moment, Sam was worried the boy would shout out and get him in trouble. *In trouble with whom, though?* Sam still had no idea where he was. His recollection only brought him as far as being snatched up by that stupid witch.

Sam and the boy on the second level stood staring at each other for several moments. He had a worrisome expression on his face, calling out to Sam with his subtle, but unquestioningly scared, expression. *I promise I'll send help*, Sam thought to himself.

With those thoughts, Sam gathered up small bouts of energy to take one step and then another. Sam trudged in slow movements along the muddy path of the Watcher's deep, underground cavern. He marched beyond the large wooden tree house of levers and into the shadows. Darkness engulfed him.

Sam, feeling as weak as ever, wished he were back in his bed, with his two best friends. If only Emmy and Jack were there, he knew he could escape. When the three of them were together, anything was possible.

Sliding along the perpetual cavern wall, head spinning and knees weak, Sam squinted and saw the smallest ray of light up ahead.

Using his hands as his guide, he continued forward, the light growing with each step.

Operating on low battery, Sam labored on, as he approached the lit-up clearing. Head hanging low and obstructed from view, Sam observed.

There was a rather large creature. A monster, even. He was the biggest organism Sam had ever seen in his twelve short years of life. The creature bore skin similar to a reptile, with green and purple scales radiating on his bulbous bones. Its gargantuan frame was topped by a head the size of a watermelon and cascaded with rippling muscles like giant beach balls. The monster's face was elongated by a giant snout, alligator-like eye pockets, and teeth that were white pencils in sharp rows. Many sharp rows.

Even worse than the monster's appearance was the clearing itself. Looking around, careful not to be seen, Sam observed clocks everywhere. His head tired again, as the room spun slightly. Bouts of dizziness came in waves. Clocks on the walls, clocks on the floor. In fact, the throne this dinosaur of a monster sat on was made up entirely of clocks. The room buzzed with ticks and tocks.

Through his dizzy haze, Sam could only think of one thing, and one thing only: *the Watcher.*

8

Emmy and Jack squished along the cavern they had chosen, leading to who knows where. "This is too bizarre," Jack said.

"Stay focused, dingus."

"I am focused!" Jack replied.

"It's okay if you're scared. We did just see a witch."

"Well, I'm not scared."

"Oh, really? Because I am," Emmy said.

"Yeah, I guess I am, too," Jack replied.

Using whatever light their eyes had adjusted to, Jack and Emmy shared a glance, hugged, and kept moving forward.

"How are we ever going to find Sam in here?" Jack asked tiredly.

"I don't know, Jack. But we need to keep going forward, there's no turning back no—" Before she finished her thought, a low rumble interrupted her.

"What was that?" Jack said.

"I don't know, but I don't want to find out."

Emmy and Jack looked around the dimly lit cavern in search of the origins of the rumble. Everything seemed calm.

"Let's keep going. I think it's gone," Emmy said as the rumbling subsided.

They only made it a few more steps before the rumbling came back even stronger.

"I don't like this at all," Jack said.

The pair started walking at a much faster pace. The farther along they traveled into the muddy depths of the cavern, the darker it became. Their eyes were no longer able to adjust because it was so dark.

The rumbling had grown considerably with their most recent steps.

"I think it's getting closer, hold my hand!" Jack said.

Emmy couldn't see enough at this point to even make out where Jack was standing. She circled around several steps trying to grab Jack's hand.

Remembering her cell phone, Emmy reached into her back pocket and whipped it out. She turned on the light to see in tunnel vision. She shone it up ahead and saw nothing. The ground was thick, a boggy creek of sludge. It was that moment that Emmy realized how cold it was down there as well.

Emmy was about to refocus the light to grab Jack's hand when she noticed something at the tail end of it, far down the cavern in front of her. "What the heck is that?" Emmy called out to Jack.

"Shine the light on it better, Emmy!" Jack looked longingly down the wide cavern corridor.

Emmy fumbled with the phone in her hands, a nervous Nellie. Finally getting the field of light directly on the incoming object, Emmy spoke. "It kind of looks like a rock."

"You're right!" Jack said. "Is it me, or does it seem to be rolling directly toward us?"

The object looked like a small stone the size of a baseball. Slowly, the stone thing rolled right along, splishing and splashing in the gunk of the floor. The stone trudged up and through the muddy trenches that lay in front of them.

Emmy and Jack kept their eyes laser focused on the shape approaching them. Not knowing how to act, how to proceed, they stood transfixed. The low rumble was a heavy buzzing now. Emmy and Jack looked at each other once, then back at the stone rolling toward them.

"What do I do, dingus?!" Emmy called out to Jack. "It's coming right for me!"

Jack looked on as the stone was rapidly reaching Emmy. "Um, UM . . ." Jack, panicking, fumbled his words. "We need to . . ." And before Jack even had a chance to finish his thought, and although it didn't have legs, the stone managed to leap into the air and clomp down onto Emmy's foot.

"OWWWW!" Emmy cried out in a shrill scream of hurt as the rumble came to life in the distance, as an army of stone things came rolling from beyond the darkness and into their field of vision.

"RUN!" Jack screeched. And with his words, Jack grabbed Emmy's hand, and the two raced off down the corridor they had originally careened down, Emmy with a slight hitch in her step from where the stone clomped her.

"Whatever you do, don't stop running!" Jack called out to Emmy.

"Copy that, dingus!" And the two ran at top speed, the fire quickly filling up their lungs. Both kids were mostly athletic, but they had never needed to run for their lives before. The air in their lungs was quickly used up out of necessity, and their lower bodies felt like Jell-O. They pumped their legs as fast as they could, and neither looked back in fear.

"Up ahead! The clearing!" Emmy called, just able to make out the clearing they had arrived in up ahead in the distance. Emmy was able to see the endless caverns circling around the main clearing where they had first entered the cave.

Although the two friends were huffing now, their chests heaving in rapid succession, up and down, a slight relief washed over them as they realized they might have a chance. Reaching the clearing, Emmy looked around. Thousands of caverns rested all around them. *If this is behind door number one*, Emmy thought, *who knows what else is in this place?*

Emmy quickly spotted the shoelace lining they had left down the corridor they came in. "This way!" She said, and the two of them ran back down the cave they had first arrived in.

Emmy and Jack took five giant leaps into the cavern, darkness swallowing them as the rumble erupted into the clearing.

"Shhhh," Jack whispered. The two looked on as the masses of rolling stones trudged through the sludgy clearing. It was incredible. There must have been hundreds of those things.

Holding hands, the two watched from the dark shadows of one of the many corridors down in the secret underground lair. The stone things paraded through and on into another long hallway for what felt like an eternity.

"Look at those things," Emmy called out.

"Shhhh!" Jack responded, using his hands to emphasize the dangerous predicament they were in.

More just kept rolling on through. Stone after stone, they rolled. And when the last stone finally passed, Emmy and Jack looked at each other, still holding hands. It was at this moment they realized that things would never be the same again. Emmy took one look around the clearing, the blackness in the many long corridors that surrounded them, and she gripped Jack's hand even tighter.

"For Sam?" she said.

"For Sam," Jack replied.

The two began walking.

9

In his dazed state, Sam watched in true horror. Could this really be? The Watcher? Right in front of his eyes? It all added up, it had to be. The clocks, the underground cavern, the levers, the switches—it all made sense. The legend was true!

Sam knew his time to make a move was short. He felt stiffness creeping in all over his body. The longer he remained down there, the worse it got. Whatever the Watcher had done to him had left him lifeless, an empty void. His brain and head felt fuzzy and weak. It was increasingly hard for Sam to put together coherent thoughts. Other than the fear that settled in all over, the only thing his body and mind were capable of putting together as coherent thoughts were his two best friends, Emmy and Jack.

Sam creeped another step toward the Watcher and collapsed to the ground, out of sight and in the darkness. *"I need you guys, now more than ever,"* Sam whispered to himself, as a tear trickled out of his eye, down his cheek, and then dropped to the muddy floor.

The Watcher instantly snapped his head in Sam's direction. He didn't know exactly what, but he sensed something just beyond the shadows, coming from Sam's direction. The Watcher's eyes honed in on the darkness, of whatever he sensed coming from Sam's direction. Sam's teardrop had raised a slight suspicion in the Watcher, as he had senses beyond normal capacity. The Watcher stood up from his throne of clocks, stretching his massive frame out to full length.

"Whoooooo goooeesss thereeee?!" The Watcher roared to life with his words, crashing one fist on the ground as he spoke. All around him, the cave erupted into vibrations. Several clocks that lined his cave fell to the ground.

Sam, terrified, wiped away another tear that had formed in the corner of his eye and did his best to keep himself hidden in the darkness. Sam pushed himself back against the cavern wall excruciatingly well. His back and shoulders were numb from pushing so hard.

"Shoowwwww yourseellffff!!" The Watcher shrieked and took two more behemoth steps over to where Sam was hiding.

I'm done; this is the end, Sam thought to himself.

At that moment, Sam felt a tingling sensation on his left arm, which was pinned back in fear against the wall of the cave. Although the darkness made it hard to see, a rather large and cruddy insect had decidedly made its way onto Sam's hand. Sam wasn't exactly sure you could call it an insect, as it was roughly four inches in length, and from what Sam could see, it didn't look like anything he had ever seen before.

The thing crawling on Sam's arm moved like a

caterpillar, oozing along, back to front, but it didn't look like one. Its main body was made up of thousands of tiny black bulbs that kind of looked like blueberries. Leveled out sporadically through the blueberries were giant green spikes. At its head, the insect looked out from four red, bulbous eyes.

Sam felt it nuzzle a tiny bit farther up his hand and make its way onto his arm. He couldn't scream; the Watcher was too close now. He knew this would be the end of him, but he cupped a hand to his mouth to stop himself from making a noise.

The Watcher took another vibrating step toward where Sam was hiding in the stillness of his cave. He still seemed so far away to Sam, but the massive stretch of the Watcher's arm closed the gap immediately, as the Watcher reached his long tendril out to Sam.

The Watcher's icy grip slowly lunged out for whatever it had thought it had heard in the darkness. It crept past the light and just beyond, into the dark lip of Sam's vicinity, when a light crash and a plump knock on the ground swept away the Watcher's attention. His gaze immediately shifted back to the light where his throne of clocks resided.

"Master, master! We need to hang this one up! It's so beautiful, indeed, this one is!" An extremely round, crusty, grotesque, blue creature had grabbed the Watcher's attention. She had tripped on her own two feet, and the clock she was holding crashed to the floor.

"Bramildaaa, youuu foolll!" The Watcher looked on in anger at Bramilda the clumsy witch's incompetence.

His attention completely wavered from Sam, and the Watcher fee-fi-fo-fummed back to his throne to meet Bramilda, and the peculiar clock she was holding that crashed to the floor.

"I think it's ready, master. The boy is coming along nicely. He's twisting, turning, and soon enough, he will be ours FOREVER!" Bramilda picked up the clock that she had dropped to the floor and handed it to her master.

The Watcher snatched it from Bramilda the witch's veiny hand, knocking her over in the process. Bramilda and Gramilda were twins, although one donned a green, scaly skin and the other a blue, shiny exterior. The witch twins were also as deviously evil as they were clumsy.

Nonetheless, the witch twins were the Watcher's top-two henchwomen and did his evilest bidding. As long as Gramilda and Bramilda, the clumsy witches, were around, no child was safe from the clutches of the evilest being that ever lived, the Watcher himself.

The Watcher picked up the clock that Bramilda had dropped and held it up to the light. It pulsed, breathing in and out. "Ahh, yess." The Watcher rumbled. A delicate smile formed on his scaly snout.

The Watcher took one heavy, deep breath in and whooshed out a breath that was instantly consumed back into the clock. He did this a few more times, breathing in and out. His breath radiated back into the clock, making it swell, a balloon being pumped with helium.

Sam resided just out of the Watcher's and Bramilda's

fields of vision in darkness. He looked on in horror and felt himself fading as the Watcher breathed his essence into the clock. With each breath the Watcher gave to the clock, Sam felt an existential rush of dread. It felt to him like someone was pulling the wind from his lungs and the thoughts from his brain. His peripheral vision waned, and his brain felt unable to focus.

On and on the Watcher went, breathing out misty billows of Sam's essence into the clock, draining him more and more with each whoosh.

In his dazed state, Sam kept his gaze longingly at the Watcher and Bramilda. He focused on the clock in the Watcher's hands. Whatever energy Sam had left was completely gone, sucked out of him. He wanted badly to stand up, go over, and rip the clock out of the Watcher's hand and launch it against the wall, but it was too late for him. The Watcher had sucked him dry. He knew now, he had figured it out. The Watcher was slowly sucking the life force, his soul, from him and storing it in that very clock.

Unable to feel much of anything now, Sam noticed the blueberry insect now crawling up ahead in his line of sight. It must have crawled off and left him in peace. When, he did not know. His vision was locked in one place and his mind and body transfixed.

The next thing he saw was more disgusting than anything else. The grotesque, blue witch bent down low, cowering her head to the floor. Her tongue slopped out, growing in length to what must have been an entire foot long. Working to slurp up the blueberry insect,

Bramilda slipped and landed belly down, her tongue creeping back into her mouth. The witch then lay on the cold cavern floor, staring directly eye to eye with the insect, and she savaged it up off the ground. Black bug bits and juicy extremities bounced all around her face. A giant smirk formed there.

Sam's eyelids felt droopy. Like the rest of his body, everything was shutting down. Soon enough, he would be at the complete mercy of the Watcher and his underground gang of henchmen and women. Free to bid their will and help work the giant clock tower that he escaped from.

The Watcher let out one last, long whoosh of essence into the clock he was holding.

Sam's clock was now a watermelon, radiating a glow of energy. He felt the pulsing of the clock, in and out and up and down. It seemed to be alive. It thumped within the Watchers' massive hands like a heartbeat. The clock was full of life, now. It was full of Sam's life, and there it would remain forever. Or so he thought. No child had ever escaped the clutches of the Watcher.

Sam had no choice but to give up. He shut his eyes and gave in to the awesome display of power from the Watcher. Sam's last thought before his eyes closed were his two best friends, Emmy and Jack.

10

Emmy and Jack began their retreat, away from the rolling stones that had preceded them. Step by step, they moved farther down the dark cave.

"Welp, the good news is we already covered one cavern down here," Emmy said.

"Yep, only three million left to go," Jack replied, chuckling.

"Oh, perfect. We'll be done in a jiffy."

"I don't care how many caverns there are down here, or how long it takes us. I don't care if we *never* see the light of day again. That hag took Sam. We don't leave here until we find him. Kapeesh?"

"Kapeesh, dingus breath," Emmy responded. Before speaking again, Emmy looked over at Jack, who was staring down at the ground as he walked, hands in his pockets. "Hey, Jack?"

Jack looked up from his fixed stare and up at Emmy. "Hmm?"

"We will find him. And we're gonna have Halloween

sleepovers, and watch scary movies, and eat all kinds of delicious pizza."

Jack smiled at Emmy's words.

"And I'll tell you what?" Emmy continued. "You can steal all the cheese you want."

Emmy and Jack were both smiling now, laughing at the sheer magnitude of the situation. The two had no idea where they were or what to do. All they knew was that their best friend, Sam, had been captured by one ugly witch and brought somewhere among the darkest depths of this cave.

"This way," Emmy said.

"Why this way?" Jack responded.

"You got a better idea, Jackie boy?"

"This one looks better," Jack pointed at a peculiar corridor that lay just a few feet away.

"They look exactly the same, Jack!" Emmy responded.

"I suppose they do, Emmy. I suppose they do." Jack thought for a moment. "Okay, fine." He paused. "But if we get attacked by another massive gang of living rocks, I'm choosing the next one."

"There's nothing else in here, don't worry. No one's been in this place for centuries!" Emmy said convincingly, clearly unaware of just how wrong she truly was.

"If you say so, Em." Jack followed Emmy's lead, and the two began walking along the new path they had chosen. "So where do you think we are?"

"Well, if I had to guess, I would say we're in that

giant, creepy tree we came down." Emmy spoke sarcastically.

"No durr, Emmy," Jack said. "But where do you *actually* think we are? What is this place?"

Emmy and Jack continued on their path for a minute, inching along the darkness without speaking, no real plan in mind, only knowing that they needed to find their best friend, Sam.

"Do you think we're still on Earth?" Jack spoke again, a lost puppy looking for a treat.

"Will you shut it?" Emmy clapped back, frustrated. "Of course we're still on Earth. We didn't just magically leave the planet!"

"What makes you so sure about that?" Jack said.

Before Emmy even had a chance to respond, her steps began to gunk and squish even more. The ground was again turning into a thick mud. "Ew, what is this?" Emmy yelled.

"Shhh, don't yell too loud. Something tells me we're not alone down here," Jack, scared, replied.

The floors of the cave were growing thicker and wetter with each step. Their feet were getting stuck and suctioned to the floor. One foot after another. *Squish, gunk, squish, gunk*. Their feet were getting harder to pull up with each step, the jelly beneath pulling their heels down.

"The mud is getting thicker," Jack said. "I'm having trouble walking.

"I know, it's like we're in a swamp or something," Emmy replied.

Emmy and Jack's steps were slowing down tremendously, the thick, viscous substance beneath an obstacle to their finish line.

Slower and slower the pair walked, trying their best to lift each foot up, one at a time.

"My feet hurt, Emmy. This mud is exhausting. We should head back and try a different corridor. I can't see anything, it's too dark!" Jack complained.

"We can't go back now, Jack. We've already come too far down here. We can do this. I believe in us." And on the pair went.

The goo they were walking in became even thicker. The two were barely able to lift their feet with each step, the jelly serving as a glue and the heels of their feet sucking to the floor. Emmy pulled out her phone light to see what the gluey, jellylike substance was, keeping the light on low to preserve the battery life.

"Look at this place!" Emmy, seeing the full picture of the cavern, spoke out.

"Holy moly!" Jack responded. "What is it?" he wondered aloud.

The light of the phone was dim, so Emmy and Jack were just barely able to make out their surroundings. But when they finally laid eyes on what surrounded them, they stood mouths agape.

All around them, the two witnessed a swirl of magical colors. Purples, pinks, reds, and yellows. Some areas were highlighted by just one color of gunk, but others the colors swirled together into a Picasso of colored jellies.

"This is incredible! What do you think this is?!" Jack spoke, in awe at the heavy, colorful substances and gunk that revolved all around them.

Emmy gazed around longingly for a moment, taking in her new environment before responding.

"WHOA" was all Emmy could say at first, followed by brief silence, her mouth open in awe. "What the heck is it?"

"I'm not exactly sure, but something smells delicious!" A whiff of something spectacular had begun teasing Jack's nostrils.

"What? I don't smell anyth—" And before she finished her sentence, the aroma hit Emmy like a brick shattering a glass window. It smashed right through her. "—ing." Emmy's eyes closed in delight.

"That smells unbelievable!" Jack said. "It smells like grapes!"

"And peaches!" Emmy replied.

"And blueberries!"

"And strawberries!"

Emmy and Jack became lost in a river of sensational aromas that filled their body up right to their cores. It was unlike anything they had ever seen or smelled before. It swept them off their feet.

The smell that was now consuming both of their palates was tantalizing their senses, distracting them from the task at hand.

"I think I'm in heaven, Jack. This is the most delicious smell I've ever smelled." Emmy perked up and looked around with her flashlight. The cavern walls were completely colorful now. Shades of the colored goo heavily lined the walls that stood all around them. It was dripping from everywhere.

Jack, dazed by the mesmerizing smell, sniffed around, looking for the culprit, the source of the smell. Slowly, as the goo was still glue-like on his feet, Jack lifted one foot and stepped closer to the cavern wall. *Squish, gunk*. And then his other foot, even slower. *Squish, gunk*. Jack stood gazing longingly at the cavern wall, then moved his face closer and took in one giant sniff with his nose.

"Mmmmmmm! This is it! It's the walls! I think it's jelly!" Jack realized now that they were completely engulfed in a giant cave of the freshest and most delicious-smelling jelly they had ever seen.

"Let me smell!" Emmy followed suit and walked over to the opposite cave wall, keeping her phone light on the entirety of the cave. *Squish, gunk, squish, gunk* she went. One step at a time, slowly making her way over to the opposite cavern wall.

Emmy reached out a finger, as if to scoop out a delicious taste of the jelly. A sneak trial of her birthday cake. But before her finger even touched the wall, a slop of jelly fell from the ceiling and landed right onto her face.

"URG! Wurt ge huck!" Emmy spoke through a faceful of jelly. It didn't take long for her anger to subside, as the sweet deliciousness of the jelly made its way into her mouth.

"Are you okay, Emmy?" Jack cried out.

Emmy was silent, taking her sweet time in responding, enjoying the moment and slurping away at the jelly that careened her lips.

"Emmy?!" Jack spoke again, this time with more emphasis.

Emmy turned to face Jack, her face a rainbow. The light shined directly on Jack's face. Jack could see that Emmy had a giant smile on hers.

"You need to try this," Emmy said and scooped a giant slab of the yumminess off the wall and into her mouth.

Without even speaking, Jack took to his own wall and went to town. Like two kids in candy shops, they devoured the jelly. First, they started scooping with their fingers, but after the first few attempts, they realized they needed more with each bite! They eventually graduated to full-hand scoops, doing their best to satiate the incredible palate for jelly they had developed.

"That was unbelievable," Jack said, leaning against the wall. His mouth and face were now also covered in the food.

"I think I'm in heaven, Jack. I really do. I've never tasted anything like that in my life. Maybe we really *are* on another planet," Emmy said.

"Okay, now back to our plan at hand," Jack said.

"Wait, what was our plan, again?" Emmy said.

"Our plan, our plan." Jack sounded confused. "Oh, right! We were down here looking for something!" Jack cried out.

"Yes, that's right! What the heck were we looking for?" Emmy responded.

A brief moment of silence was met by a yell from both friends at the same exact time.

"SAM!"

11

Her attention now back to finding Sam, Emmy went to take one step forward and realized her feet wouldn't cooperate. She tried her best to lift her feet and get walking back in the right direction, but she couldn't.

"I can't move, Jack! I think I'm stuck."

Jack looked over to where his friend complained. "It's the jelly! Just lift your feet up one at a time!"

Emmy tried again, but her feet simply wouldn't budge. Her left foot had sunk quite a bit farther down than her right. "I can't move, Jack. Come back and help me."

Jack looked back over to where Emmy was standing. It took massive amounts of willpower for him to move away from the wall whose smells had transfixed his attention. Jack took in a deep breath and a giant sniff of the wall before making his move.

"All right, fine. I guess I'll help you," Jack said, lifting one foot with great difficulty. *Squish*, his foot came up off the ground. *Gunk*, it landed back down one foot ahead. Jack then tried to lift his other foot but found that he could not. "Uh, Emmy? I guess this is not the best time to tell you that I'm also stuck."

Panic rose in both Emmy's and Jack's bodies. Their feet locked into the ground, a vice grip keeping them in place.

"Maybe try lifting with your hands!" Jack called out to Emmy.

Emmy took the suggestion, pitting both of her arms underneath her right leg.

Jack took his own advice as well, getting his arms ready to pull up on his right leg.

"Okay, on three," Emmy said.

"One," Jack said.

"Two," Emmy responded.

"THREE!" they both said at the same time.

As soon as the words exited their mouths, an uproarious mountain of gargling goo rumbled and rose up not far from where they were standing. The best friends looked on in horror at the gargantuan thing that had materialized right in front of them.

"Jack, help!" Emmy screamed out.

Jack wanted to help, but his eyes were locked on the incredible thing that had risen from the jelly. He wanted to run, as fast as he could away from this cave, away from the monster in front of him, but he had never seen anything like this in his life. He couldn't look away.

The monster that rose was roughly twelve feet high and dawned all the way to the top of the cavern ceiling. It had no visible limbs or features on its body, just a mountain of colored goo and gunk, cascading down its volcanic body. Eruptions of various colors of jelly oozed out from every section, many volcanoes erupting.

The most horrifying thing was what Jack noticed above the creature's body.

"Jack, watch out!" Emmy screamed. Although the jelly monster had no limbs or body parts, a widened grin and yellow eyes were staring at the two from its ugly mug.

The jelly monster opened its mouth, let out a long and menacing roar, and then choked out a wad of hideous, black goo that came flying at Jack.

Thinking quickly, Jack leaped out of his shoes, which were stuck to the gooey cavern floor. He landed on all fours about three feet away, quickly turning back to see what was flung his way.

The black goo was a direct hit where Jack was standing prior. It landed on his shoes and momentarily sat there covering them. Seconds after, a hiss of smoke rose from them, melting Jack's shoes into nothing.

"Emmy, your shoes! Lose the shoes!" It was easy for Jack to leap out of them because the two had already taken the laces out earlier. "Now, Emmy!"

The jelly monster turned its attention over to where Emmy stood in shock, unable to move.

"Now, Emmy! LOSE YOUR SHOES!" Jack quickly grabbed a slop of the tasty goo from the wall and tossed it at Emmy's face.

GOOSH! It landed and hit her point blank, waking her from her stupor.

"Emmy, lose your shoes!" Jack called out again.

Now that his attention was directly on Emmy, the jelly monster reared its head once again and prepared to let out a wad of the poisonous black jelly.

As the jelly monster did so, Emmy leaped out of her shoes, evading the attack and landing right into Jack's arms. The two held each other's embrace for a brief moment.

"Emmy, the jelly! We have to keep our legs moving up and down! Keep running and pumping up and down! High knees, high knees! We can't let our feet get stuck."

"Let's go!"

And the two had their plan.

Lifting their legs up and up, the two raced on toward the jelly monster. "Around it!" Emmy said. "I think we can sneak around it. Just keep pumping your legs!"

Jack nodded in agreement, and off they raced.

When they finally closed in on where the jelly monster was, ready to flank around his side for their escape, in a rumble he sunk back down into the depths of the cavern. Poof, he was gone.

The calmness was eerie for Emmy and Jack.

Emmy looked around for where the jelly monster went.

"Feet, Emmy! Keep moving your feet!"

Emmy snapped back quickly and began running in place, doing her best to keep her feet off of the gooey ground.

Huffing, Emmy called out, "Where do you think it

went?"

Jack also was breathing heavily, in and out. Pumping their legs repeatedly was tiresome. "I have no idea, but let's not wait around to find out."

Emmy and Jack ran through the rainbow cavern of delicious smells, pumping their legs high in the air.

"Up ahead!" Jack yelled, barely able to make out words; he was out of breath.

Emmy saw exactly what Jack was referring to. Another cavern was up ahead and to the right. "Let's do it!" Emmy said.

The two were just shy of the turn-off when the jelly monster rose from the ground once again, a fuming volcanic mass.

"Jack, watch out!" Emmy screamed, as the jelly monster spit out another wad of the poisonous black goo.

Jack dove out of the way, grabbing Emmy's hand in the process, and the two ran down the turn-off and far out of the jelly monster's sight.

12

The Watcher held the clock that now housed Sam's life force, his soul high up in the air. Feeling above himself, beyond powerful, in one long bellow, he let out a gargantuan laugh.

"AH HA HA HA HA HA." The cavern vibrated with each syllable.

Bramilda then joined him as well. "He he he he he he." The distinct cackle of a witch.

"Now go, Bramilda. You've done well. Go find that clumsy sister of yours and bring me more! More children. I want more children!" The Watcher was glowing now. A green aura had surrounded him, radiating from the power consumed from Sam's life force.

"Yes, master. Of course, master!" Bramilda waved her arms in the air in triumph.

Bramilda took only one step away from the Watcher before hesitating, turning her disgusting, black-hatted head to the far end of the cavern.

Bramilda lifted her face high into the air and sniffed once to make sure she wasn't crazy, and a second time as concrete confirmation.

"Master, I smell something foul," Bramilda said, turning fully around now.

Bramilda scanned the area. She took one step to the right and lifted her nose again for a good whiff. "I think it's coming from over there—"

"Oh, Bramilda, I love watching you work!" the Watcher roared.

"No, no. Wait. It's coming from over there." Bramilda cocked her head in the opposite direction now.

Taking one step and then another, she confirmed. "Yes, it's clear now, master." Bramilda scurried with her nose high in the air, sniffing away.

Bramilda reached her decrepit hand through the darkness in the entrance to the Watcher's lair and pulled out Sam, who had been lying down, next to lifeless. "Well, look what I found, master."

The Watcher instantly rose from his throne of clocks and let out a nasty rumble.

Bramilda held the boy up by the back of his pajama collar, so that he was facing the Watcher directly in the face.

"You are brave, little one," the Watcher said, staring at Sam's empty vessel. "It's a shame that you're too late."

13

Jack and Emmy stopped and dropped to the floor, far out of sight and mind from the gelatinous volcano of goo that had attacked them.

"What *was* that?" Jack said.

"I don't know, but he sure tasted good," Emmy replied.

Jack heard her response and couldn't believe she was joking after almost being destroyed by the jelly monster. After a slight moment's hesitation, Jack, too, realized the hilarity of it all and displayed a big smile.

"He did taste good, didn't he!?"

Jack and Emmy shared a good, hearty laugh, despite the fact that they were almost mauled by a ravenous pile of jelly.

"Did you get a taste of the peach jelly?" Emmy said, her mouth watering.

"It was delectable! Did you try the grape!?" Jack clapped back.

"Yes, it was molto delizioso!" Emmy kissed her hand

and waved into the air, as she spoke. An Italian chef fawning over her magnificent cuisine.

"Hey, Jack?" Emmy said.

"Yeah, Em?" Jack responded, his laughter dwindling down.

"Thanks," Emmy said.

"For what?" Jack responded.

"I froze, dude. I couldn't move. The sight of that thing, it got me. You snapped me out of it. If it weren't for you, I'd be jelly meat." Emmy locked eyes with Jack, then quickly turned away.

"Emmy, of course. You'd do the same for me. And who knows, you might have to. There's no telling what other monsters could be down here." Jack looked down at his bare feet, the ground now solid. No more jelly.

"Do you think we'll ever get out of here?" Emmy looked around. They had only traveled down a few caves at this point, among the millions they had laid eyes on when they first entered, but they had already been through so much. The possibilities were endless.

"Of course, we'll get out of here. We have to. There's a Halloween sleepover at Sam's house waiting for us." Jack grabbed Emmy's hand, and the two hugged and stood up.

Now walking barefoot, Emmy and Jack moved along down the new dark cavern they had stumbled into.

"At least the ground is solid," Emmy said.

"Yeah, and dry," Jack responded. "I do wish I could have one more taste of that jelly, though."

"Oh, well, how about we go back then, dingus?"

Emmy said, turning around to face Jack.

"I mean, sure. We just have to remember to keep pumping our legs becau—" Jack didn't get a chance to finish his sentence before Emmy cut him off.

"Hey, look!" Emmy noticed something out of the corner of her eye.

Jack looked straight ahead to where Emmy was pointing, but he was not able to make out anything in the darkness. Although the cave was slightly brighter than the one with the jelly, the rainbow colors of the goo had helped illuminate the walls.

"Look, it's right over there. On the ground!" Emmy said accusingly.

"Where, Em? I don't see a thing—" But then Jack saw it.

A small rolling stone, much like they had seen previously in the cave among the sea of stones rolling on through the cavernous trenches.

"It's one of those stones!" Jack said. "Let's go, run!" Jack quickly rushed to haul away on his bare feet. Jack ran for about five seconds before he realized that not only Emmy wasn't running with him, but that there was no sea of rolling rocks. It was just one; this particular stone was alone.

"What do you want from us?" Emmy, still staring, never taking her gaze from the stone, said.

The stone was rolling at a snail's pace along darkness of the dry cavern floor, careful not to inch too close to Emmy and Jack. The thing was moving with intention.

"Hello?" Emmy called out again. "Can you hear

me?" Emmy's words echoed off the cavern walls.

The stone had now stopped its slow-moving roll forward, and it froze. A silver ghost in the shadowy darkness.

"Where are your friends now?" Emmy called out to the stone. "Come on, then! This time, we're ready for you ugly buggers!" Emmy yelled even louder now. "We already beat you, we beat that stupid jelly monster, and now we're coming for our best friend, Sam!" Emmy hadn't realized it, but she was angry, yelling directly at the stone as if it were to blame for all of this. As if it were alive, a thing with a mind of its own. Its own thoughts, feelings, and emotions.

Slowly, with each rise in Emmy's voice, the stone creature backed away, hiding itself behind the lip of the cavern wall. Slowly, it made itself visible again with a crawl out behind the cavern wall.

"What, are you scared, you stupid stone?" Emmy called out again, her anger subsiding somewhat.

The stone again rolled back behind the wall at the sound of Emmy's voice.

"Emmy, shhh," Jack said. "I think it's scared."

"Scared? It's a freaking stupid rock! How can it be scared?" Emmy said, looking from Jack back over to where the stone was now again whimpering, out from the lip of the wall.

Relaxed, calmly lowering her voice, Emmy spoke. "Okay, Jack says you're scared, so let's start over."

The stone crept out once again, apparently wanting to be seen.

"Hi, Stony, my name is Emmy. This is Jack."

The stone rolled a few inches farther along, closer now to Emmy and Jack.

"Stony?" Jack said.

"Yeah, you got a better name for it?" Emmy argued.

"How about 'stupid stone dude'?"

"Oh yeah, that's great. The thing is already deathly afraid of us. Let's start calling it stupid stone dude." Emmy rattled back at Jack, giving him a look that said, *Shut up*.

The stone had instinctively rolled back somewhat from the minor quarrel between the best friends.

Emmy turned around and gave her undivided attention back to the stone.

"Hey, Stony." Emmy looked back at Jack as she said its name. "Hi there, little guy!"

Stony inched up closer to where Emmy was standing, and the two shared a moment of silence.

Emmy spoke again. "Are ya hungry?"

"It's not a dog, Emmy!" Jack quietly yelled at Emmy.

"Shhh." Emmy waved Jack off.

Getting on her knees, Emmy tried to communicate again. "Hi, little guy. What are you doing down here?" Emmy reached out her hand, a human longing to pet her dog.

"Come on, little guy. You can do it." Emmy was now hunched over, fully extending her arm, and Stony rolled even closer. They were mere inches away from making contact when a loud vibration shook the walls of the cave, interrupting the moment.

"Um, Em?" Jack said. "I think that's our signal to get out of here."

Emmy snapped her hand back and looked around at the vibrating walls. *What on earth is this place?* she thought to herself.

When she directed her attention back to Stony, he was not where she had left him. Stony had speedily rolled back much farther down the corridor, clearly in fear of whatever the vibration had been.

"Let's go, Em!" Jack yelled over the vibration of the cavern.

Emmy did not take her gaze off of Stony as Jack grabbed her arm and hastily pulled her up. She kept it fixed as she stood up.

Snapping back to reality, standing up she motioned to Jack. "All right, let's bust out of this joint."

Emmy and Jack, bare feet and all, ripped down the corridor, their legs pumping up and down, trying to make it as far away from the thunderous vibrations as they could. Before they turned the corner down another deep and dark cave, Emmy took one long look back down to where Stony was.

Peeking out from behind a dark cavern lip, Stony stared back.

14

"Takeee himmmmm," the Watcher roared. "Takeee thee filthyyy childdd nowww. Gett himmm outt of myy sighttt." With a flick of his wrist, and a point in the direction of the clock tower, the Watcher made his intentions clear. "Putt himmmm tooo workkk. Justttt likee three resttt of themmm!" A hearty laugh escaped him.

"Yes, master!" Bramilda, still holding Sam by his shirt collar, dragged him away, whisking him out of the Watcher's line of vision and into the deep recesses of another dark cavern.

Sam was a colorless vessel. His mind and body had merged into one distant place. A place far from where he actually, physically resided. His thoughts gone, his emotions a fog, and his memories shades of another life. Sam's body was milky white, all the color drained from his formerly fruitful and young frame.

Underneath him, Sam knew that his body was being dragged across grime and dirt, repeatedly rubbing and bumping on rocks and gravel, but he did not feel it. He knew he was in danger, but he could not stop it. And he knew he was alone but could not help it.

"He he he he he he. This is my favorite part," Bramilda squealed.

Turning his head slowly, Sam realized that they had stopped moving. Bramilda's dragging had come to a halt. Wherever she had been taking him, they had reached it.

With a wave of her finger, Bramilda lifted Sam up into the air, his body now levitating just high enough above the dirt that his toes did not drag.

She wagged her finger, and Sam's body jerked around to face the giant structure that resided in front of him. It was massive.

A giant clock tower.

Sam had been here once before, but he had had enough energy to leave. It wasn't long before the Watcher and one of the twins snatched him back up and sucked the remaining life force he had left, and they were storing it in one of those clocks.

The structure was nothing short of spectacular. It reached high up into the unseen sky, way past anything visible. There were billions and billions of levers, pulleys, and switches. At the very top, high above any height that could be deemed a reality, a glowing light illuminated it all.

Perhaps even worse than the large wooden clock tower were the children. Hundreds of children just like Sam could be seen lifting their arms, pulling them down, turning the switches, motionless and lifeless vessels doing the Watcher's evil bidding. Sam knew he was once again going to suffer the same fate.

With each shift of Bramilda's finger, Sam moved closer to the tower. He floated on, restlessly staring off into the abyss of the clock tower.

Sam wanted to scream for his parents, to call out to Jack and Emmy, but he could not. He could not muster the energy to speak, let alone yell.

"Just a little bit farther, filthy boy, he he he he he." Bramilda the witch was glowing with excitement. Her laughter faded into sheer bliss.

Bramilda continued her magic, effortless. Moving Sam with a simple tug or twist of her finger, in the direction of the clock tower where he would meet the same fate as the rest of the children down in the Watcher's underground lair of clocks.

Sam finally was close enough to the clock tower to see all the children, his fellow prisoners, up close. He wasn't able to look fully around, or too far up, but he was able to set his sights on some of the children working the clock tower.

Their milky, pale frames must have been a far cry from how they once appeared. The children wore all different types of clothing; some wore pajamas, some wore jeans and button-downs, some were barefoot, and some wore sneakers. This must have been what they were wearing when they were captured by the Watcher and his evil monsters.

Something else struck Sam's attention among the sea

of children and their horrible appearances. Some looked paler and frailer than others, almost as if they were slowly dwindling away, getting thinner, their skin graying with a silvery tone. Heavy bags and swollen, lifeless eyes donned every single one. *Do they even sleep? Do they eat?* Sam thought to himself, realizing he would probably find out the answers to that question very soon.

Probably the most concerning among the horrible things Sam observed of the children was the slate gray decay that donned some of their skin. It was rocky and scaly, and it had started to creep into the space between their fingers and their nostrils, hardening their soft heads of hair, and covering them in hideous ways all over. Although many seemed to be the same soulless, non-energy-wielding, milky pale vessels as Sam, a newly added addition to the Watcher's team, others, the rocky, scaly ones, seemed to have it worse. Something was happening to them, something evil. Sam realized these are the children that had been down there the longest.

Would the same thing happen to Sam? Sam wanted badly to help all the children being kept as slaves. He felt helpless and at the same time like he had let down an entire army of children who needed his help. Unfortunately for Sam, he was no longer in any condition to do anything to put a stop to the Watcher, the evil twin witches, and whatever else was lurking down in that horrible place.

No, I will find a way, Sam thought to himself. *There HAS to be a way*. Sam was never one to give up, and now that his fate and seemingly the fate of all these children was on his plate, he knew he had to figure something out.

"Here we are, filthy young Samuel, he he he he," Bramilda called out.

Sam's mind had wandered; his field of vision had been lost while observing the other children. He came to a subtle stop. Magically, his hand lifted into the air, and a rather large wooden lever was waiting for him. Down, he pulled. Then up, he pushed. Down, then up, then down again. Sam had reached his place among the other slaves.

"Ooouuuuuhhhh, delightful, he he he he he," Bramilda said, clapping her hands together. "Make yourself comfortable, filthy boy, he he he he he. You're going to be here for a long time, child."

Sam's arm continued down a pull, then up a push, down a pull, and then up a push.

"You're going to be here, FOREVER, HE HE HE HE HE!"

15

"I've officially had it with this place," Jack said.

Emmy stared longingly down at her bare feet, lost in a sea of thoughts.

"First, a witch. Then, an army of evil, rolling rocks. And how can we forget about the jelly monster, or the fact that we just tried to talk to one of those stupid rocks!"

"Stony," Emmy said. "His name is Stony."

"Uh, Earth to Emmy? Who cares what his name is?" Jack said.

"I do, and his name is Stony."

"You're acting weird."

Emmy broke her stare and looked up at Jack. "Yeah, whatever. Let's go find Sam."

"Yes, let's," Jack said. "Anything to get us one step closer and out of this dump."

The two best friends, missing their significant other Sam, walked on mostly in silence through several dark caverns in the underground cave. However, the most peculiar thing was that while each dark and gloomy hallway felt more or less the same, subtle differences highlighted each cavern. Some were sludgy while others were dry. Some had rocky walls while others were smooth. Some were littered with insects and nasties while others were quiet, libraries daring their visitors to make a noise. Jack and Emmy knew that their mission was only just beginning, but they also knew that it was the most important mission of their lives. They had to find Sam.

Coming to a fork in the cave, Jack broke the silence and spoke out. "Which way, Em?"

Emmy looked to her right. The cavern that stared back at her wasn't as dark as some others. There were bits of light jutting out, poking through in spots. The cave also seemed to have a touch of color, purple and green tints littered certain sections of the wall. Then, she looked to her right. This cavern looked much darker. There wasn't much to see down it except for the slops of goop falling sporadically in pieces from the ceiling.

"I'd like to not see the jelly monster ever again." Emmy said. Jack nodded in agreement, and so the two began walking down the brighter corridor to the right.

"Hey, at least we can see down here," Jack said, his face illuminated jungle green from the wall.

"I'm not so sure I want to see," Emmy replied.

It was just a few steps later that Emmy heard the noise that stopped her dead in her tracks:

Tick. Tick. Tick. Tick. Tick.

"Did you hear that?" Emmy said to Jack.

"Hear wh—?" Before he could even respond to her question, Emmy cut him off.

"Shhh. Listen."

Emmy grabbed Jack's hand and pulled him up toward the sound. It grew louder.

Tick. Tick. Tick. Tick.

"It sounds like a clock tick—"

Again, Emmy cut him off. "Shut up, dingus!" Emmy whispered, leading Jack farther toward the noise.

Emmy, still holding Jack's hand, took a few more steps toward the noise and then saw the object of their attention hanging from the top of the cave.

"Look!" Emmy called out.

"What am I looking at?" Jack said, squinting in the direction Emmy was pointing to.

"Right over there!" Emmy grabbed Jack's chin and shifted his face and eyes over to where the object she was fixated on hung from the top of the cavern.

Jack's face fell, and his mouth dropped, as he finally realized what Emmy was pointing to.

There, staring back at both Emmy and Jack, was a clock.

16

The Watcher sat on his throne of clocks, staring around the wondrous walls of ticking and tocking that surrounded him everywhere. The endless sea of clocks were breathing in and out in unity. In and out they went, the life force of all of his victims, captured over centuries of the Watcher's work.

The Watcher stood up, feeling as devious and evil as ever. He took several gigantic steps over to the wall and pressed his nose up against it, sniffing and smelling the many clocks that were lined in droves.

After sniffing quite a bit and feeling dissatisfied, the Watcher again took several gigantic steps over to a new spot on the wall. Again, he lay his nose against the many clocks, and he sniffed.

"Ahhhh, yesss. So freshhh, so ripeee." The Watcher's words echoed off the clinking and clanking that surround him. "Breakfasttt is serveddd."

The Watcher reached out and pulled down the clock he was referring to and brought it directly up to his face.

The funny thing about the Watcher's clocks is that they clung to the wall, like magnets on a fridge. There was no staple, glue, tape, or adhesive. The magic from the Watcher's incredible powers kept them there.

The Watcher took in a long, deep breath of the clock's essence, filling himself up with delight. The clock radiated.

And out the Watcher breathed, his eyes closed in pure bliss.

The Watcher continued his tactic, breathing the clock's energy in and out several more times. With each suck, the Watcher seemed to be growing, glowing, and emitting incredibly strong energy.

When he took his last breath in and blew it out, the clock was dull and lifeless. It no longer radiated a glow, and it no longer pumped in and out.

Feeling sensational, the Watcher launched the clock somewhere he did not care. It clanked against a wall and fell with a *tink*, cold and dead. The Watcher looked around, lifted his triumphant, glorious, hulking arms into the air, and bellowed his sinister laugh.

Somewhere deep in the Watcher's cavern, a small girl, who must have been seven or eight, worked a small dial back and forth. She spun it clockwise, then counterclockwise, helping to keep the clock tower's energy flowing in abundance. Before she had a chance to spin it one last time, the little girl dropped to the floor with the same *tink* as her clock had done when the Watcher had finished with it. The girl stood, staring transfixed from the ground up to the cavern ceiling, her arm still moving a dial that was no longer there. Her fingers went clockwise, then counterclockwise, still moving, locked into motion with nothing to spin. Her senses were alert; she could feel the cold of the floor on her back. She could see parts of the giant clock tower in her peripherals. She could smell the gross, arid air of the cavern all around her. But worst of all, she could hear, and what she heard made a tear trickle down her cheek. On the cold, wet ground, lying faceup in the Watcher's underground cavern of clocks and nasties, thinking about her parents, thinking about being in her warm and cozy bed, waking up to a beautiful sunny morning with her family, she heard the evilest laugh of the evilest being that had ever lived. The Watcher's laughter echoed through the entire cavern.

17

"No." Emmy's eyes were locked on the clock. They were wide with surprise and fear. "It can't be."

Jack slowly stepped over to the ticking clock that seemed to be breathing, pulsing air in and out, an infant quietly asleep in its crib.

"Don't get too close, Jack," Emmy whispered.

Jack didn't respond, only walking close enough now that he was within arm's length.

"Jack, stop!" Emmy whispered slightly louder this time.

"Shhhh." Jack met Emmy with a whispered shush of his own.

Reaching out, Jack attempted to grab the clock from the wall. Before his hand actually met the clock, a blaring vibration and alarm screamed out from it.

It took both friends a minute to fully realize what was going on, that it was no longer quiet, and their shade of safety rapidly was pulled from underneath them.

Looking at each other, Emmy yelled, "RUN!"

Jack and Emmy took off, pumping their legs again in hot pursuit, far away from the trill and *timph* of the alarm clock.

They didn't make it very far before they saw more clocks. All different types of clocks lining the walls of the cavern. They were everywhere, and it was an incredibly frightening sight.

Trying their best not to focus on the clocks all around them, Emmy and Jack continued running until the alarm was out of range.

Slowing down and out of breath, Emmy spoke. "They're everywhere!"

Jack rotated in his spot. He finally had a chance to stop and admire the magnificent sight around him. "This is incredible!"

"Yeah, incredibly horrifying, Jack," Emmy replied.

Jack was fixated on the clocks. "No, no. This is just incredible! We can make a fortune! Look at these clocks! They have to be one-of-a-kinds!" Jack walked over to one clock, careful not to be too close to set off another alarm.

The clock Jack locked in on was orange and had a green stem sticking out of the top. It had lined grooves all around, and it even smelled like a pumpkin.

"Look, Emmy. This clock is a pumpkin!" Jack was smiling as he spoke, extremely amused at their discovery.

Emmy's interest was piqued, and now she too walked over to a clock that caught her eye. This clock was a long rectangle, top to bottom. Not wide but thin and tall. It was a magnificent pink and had lavender glitter and sparkle dressing it. There were two butterfly wings jutting out from the back. The clock's face was sparkly purple.

"This is magnificent," Jack said.

"What IS this place?" Emmy said, staring at another clock now with green scales and horns creeping out of the top.

Jack thought for a moment but then stopped dead in his tracks when the realization hit him like a thick brick, right in the face.

"Emmy, you don't think?"

Emmy still staring at the scaly clock, turned her attention back to Jack. "Think what?"

"Oh, come on. The clocks, the underground cavern, all of this!" Jack said, waving his arms into the air, emphasizing the outrageous shenanigans happening all around them.

Emmy's realization didn't come as swiftly as Jack's had. "Come on, what? What are you talking ab—" But then the brick hit her just as it had Jack.

Staring at each other, glossy eyed and frightened, they both said his name at the same time:

"The Watcher."

"It can't be, Jack. It just can't be!" Emmy cried out, remaining careful not to be too loud or get too close to any of the clocks on the walls.

"It has to be, Em!" Jack responded in a whispered scream. "It just has to be. What else could it possibly be?"

"So you're telling me Sam, our best friend, the third member of our legendary trio, was captured by the Watcher?" Emmy looked longingly at Jack.

"Well, I don't know for sure, Emmy. But what I do know is that we've made it this far, and there's only one way to find out." Jack grabbed Emmy's hand and held it tight.

"We have to keep going," Emmy said.

"We need to find Sam and get out of here, and fast."

"Jack, look!" Emmy said, as she saw a large shadow creeping, looming over the wall of clocks, and heard the faintest sound of footsteps.

Emmy, hand still intertwined with Jack's, rushed him over to behind the back wall of clocks, far and out of reach from the shadow that had begun to take form. What the two saw, they didn't like.

Emmy and Jack crouched down low in a mad rush, their faces only inches apart.

Jack had never been this close to a girl before. He stared with his large blue eyes directly back into Emmy's, a moment frozen in time.

"Back up, dingus. Your breath smells like a fart," Emmy said.

The moment was lost, but Jack would remember.

Attention now shifting back to the shadow, Jack saw and heard what it had been hiding.

"La da dee dum, la da dee dom." Bramilda, the evil twin sister of Gramilda the witch, pranced along, her large feet like tennis rackets. The sound of soft thumps littered their hearing as Bramilda moved step-by-step through the bizarre cavern of clocks.

Jack gripped Emmy's hand, tightening his hold on her knuckles, turning them to white, as they looked on in fright.

Bramilda continued waddling along, her blue skin shining. A huge grin spread across her warty face, as she momentarily brought her attention to a clock on the wall. Lifting one gnarly, long-nailed digit, she magically levitated a clock down to her level. It came with ease. This particular clock was small, round, and dark black all over.

"On my way, my big fat feet. The souls of children, I'll forever eat. Become my slave and forever pay. A lifetime of misery, I dare shall say. So take this—" Bramilda stopped her incantation, like a car abruptly stopping at a red light.

Cocking her head in their direction, Emmy and Jack squeezed even tighter. Bramilda took one giant leap in their direction, peeking her head just out of reach of where the two best friends were strapped tightly to each other. Just as she was about to round the corner, Bramilda got a whiff of a large, delicious insect inching along just back over by the wall of clocks. She whipped her entire body and leaped, diving headfirst over to the ground where the blueberry, bulbous bug crawled. Bramilda, lying belly down on the ground, slurped it up in an instant and let out a grotesque burp.

Emmy wanted to barf. Jack squeezed her hand

painfully tight, begging her to hold it together. Their souls depended on it.

Bramilda, the evil witch, picked herself up, dusted off her fat bottom, and waddled away and out of sight from Emmy and Jack, letting out a cackle of her own. "He he he he he he he he."

The sound pierced both Emmy's and Jack's ears.

When they were comfortable they could no longer be seen or heard, they, too, picked themselves up and rose from behind the wall.

"I think I'm gonna be sick," Emmy said.

"If you're gonna barf, at least do it over there," Jack responded.

Emmy smiled and gave him a loving shove.

"That was a close call," Emmy said. "Let's keep going. We have to be near something."

"Yeah, if these clocks mean what I think they mean, we have to keep going."

And so on they went. Jack and Emmy grabbed each other's hands one more time, squeezed tightly, let go, and moved their attention onward and back to their mission at hand.

"Let's keep going down this way," Emmy said, pointing down the direction where Bramilda came from.

"Okay, but stay close to me. We need to stick together if we're going to make it out of here alive," Jack said.

Emmy nodded, and the two marched on in search of their best friend, Sam.

18

The Watcher, feeling as powerful as ever, stomped his massive feet through his domain. On he went through a small corridor that separated his chamber from where his children were, powering his life's work, the giant clock tower.

Making his way through the clearing, he stopped and admired it all. His slave children were hard at work, pumping, clicking, and pressing all the various tools needed for his work to be done.

The clearing opened up to the top of the clock tower, where the giant light source resided. The Watcher gazed longingly at the monstrous clock that lived there. The true source of his evil powers. A smile spread across his snout.

Looking down at all the children, hundreds of milky, chalky white vessels slaving away all for him, the Watcher felt powerful. *There is nothing, and will never be anything, as powerful and evil as me.* The Watcher lifted a long, scaly finger, and a thin ray of electricity beamed from the giant clock that sat at the top of the tower, connecting to his finger.

It was the surge of electricity that caused the Watcher to grow. In seconds, he had grown double in size, his snout elongated, new rows of sharp fangs forming behind his lips. His impossibly long, scaly, green ears stretched out to sharp points, his fingernails sharpening to razor blades. He didn't turn to its powers often, but as the years went by, he felt he needed it more and more. The energy it provided, the strength it gave him. The more children he enslaved, the more powerful he was.

The Watcher knew his mission was coming to an end soon. He knew that his powers were growing, and it wouldn't be long before he would have enough children to rise up from his underground prison to enslave all the children in the world.

The surge of electricity dwindled, and the Watcher's large barrel chest came down in succession, a runner finishing a marathon. Dozens of children working down below dropped to the floor. They were empty vessels on the outside but full of life on the inside. Their thoughts, emotions, and feelings all intact deep within, wanting badly to make their way back to the surface. But as long as the Watcher remained their master, they would never be able to.

The Watcher lifted his arms high up into the air, guillotines waiting to strike down the objects of their destruction. In one fell swoop, the Watcher's arms ripped down, and with them, a strike of lightning blasted the floor of the cave.

In the exact spot where the lightning struck, a crack in the earth was formed. Rapidly the line in the soil spread, and out rose a ray of faint, red light.

Emerging from the growing red light below were the silhouettes of three hideous monsters.

The first monster that rose was a pumpkin who looked out from yellow light within its core. Two evil slits made up its eyes, and razor-sharp cuts carved out the jagged edges of its smile. The pumpkin sat on top of a large green stalk. It walked awkwardly, its long, branchlike arms flailing about.

The second monster to rise was a mummy. The only thing visible between the ragged, dirty wraps that draped its entire body were two black eyes—the coldest eyes anyone ever saw.

The last monster to fumble its way out of the hellish red beam was a troll. A disgusting, foul-smelling, large-nosed, ooey-gooey, snotty troll. In one hand that was dripping large, green gobs of snot, he held a massive ax. In the other, a small straw sack.

All three of the Watcher's creations took in their new surroundings, looking over to the clock tower, the children, and finally up at their creator, the Watcher himself. They looked on in delight and awaited orders from their master.

"GOOO NOOOWWW, MY MINIONNSS!" The Watcher spoke triumphantly. "GOOO NOOOWWW

AND BRRINGG MEE MOREEE CHILDRENNN!! BRING ME THE SOULS OF ALLL THE CHILDRENN IN MILLL FALLSSS!!"

The pumpkin, mummy, and troll scattered off in succession, knowing there was work to be done.

Feeling his newfound power, taking a long look at his work, the master let out one of his evil laughs. "NOTHINGGG CANN STOPP MEEEE, AH HA HA HA HA." The Watcher raised his gigantic arms into the air as his laughter rained down on all of his slaves.

Unfortunately for the Watcher, he was not privy to the knowledge that two very lovable, very warm, and very kind young children were creeping their way into his main chamber at that very moment. They were missing their best friend, and there is nothing in this world or the next, no evil power, that could stand up to the incredible powers of their friendship.

19

"What was that?" Emmy said, frightened.

"It sounded like lightning. We have to keep going. Come on!" Jack started pumping his legs, making his way through the hallway of bizarre and absurd clocks they had found themselves in. Emmy followed him.

It wasn't long before Emmy and Jack reached a large clearing at the end of the hall. What they saw there trumped anything they had seen up to that point.

"Emmy, quick! Over here," Jack called to Emmy, ducking down behind the cave wall, looking out into the clearing at the monsters rising from the crack in the ground.

Emmy was about to join Jack and duck down herself to get a closer glimpse of the three monstrosities clawing up and out from where the lightning had struck the ground, but a quick glance back to the hall they came from made her stop in her tracks.

"Emmy, what is it?" Jack asked, pushing for her to join him as quickly as possible.

Emmy and Jack both looked back now and saw Stony. Again, he showed himself, rolling slowly out from behind the wall, a turtle popping out of its shell just to say hello.

"Look. It's Stony. He must have followed us all the way here," Emmy said, getting down on one knee.

"Who cares about that stupid rock, Emmy?" Jack pulled Emmy's hand and brought her over to where he was hiding.

Emmy's fixed attention was momentarily shattered. When she regained her composure and looked back at Stony, he was gone.

"Look at that!" Jack said. "This is way more important that that stupid rock."

The noises emanating from the clearing hit them immediately. The sounds of the giant clock tower—loud pops and cranks, tinks, and bangs—hit them from everywhere.

"This can't be real," Jack said. "Are you seeing the same thing I'm seeing?"

Emmy and Jack looked on as the pumpkin walking on giant green stalks, the mummy, and the troll scurried away and down the opposite side of the clearing.

Emmy and Jack then fully shifted their attention to the massive clock tower making all the noise. Focusing on the withered children lined up all over it, the realization hit them.

"Those are kids, Emmy!" Jack said. "All around the clock tower. Kids!"

"Sam has to be down here. Let's go, quickly, before it's too late! Emmy attempted to rush out into the clearing, but Jack stopped and pulled her back behind the wall.

"Not so fast," Jack said. "Look up there."

Emmy couldn't believe her eyes. They were telling her one thing, but her brain was telling her another. *This isn't possible.* There, up on a ledge, his massive frame casting a shadow down below, was the massive monstrous dinosaur-like creature, the Watcher.

"The Watcher," Emmy whispered. "It's all true, all of it! The clocks, the Watcher, it's all true! And he's got Sam!"

"Emmy, keep it together! We need to find Sam, and we need to do it now." Jack took a look at the children all around the clock tower. "By the looks of it, we need to do this fast."

"Okay, I can do this." Emmy took a deep breath in and nodded at Jack. "We can do this. Together." Emmy gripped Jack's hand.

Slowly tiptoeing out, careful not to be seen or heard, Jack and Emmy rode the edge of the wall in darkness. They knew that they needed to get closer. If Sam was anywhere to be found in this nightmare cavern, it was right there in that clearing.

From the darkness of the wall's shadow, Emmy looked around for answers. They needed to get closer to the clock tower to find Sam, but without being seen by the Watcher, who was perched atop a cliff roughly fifty feet up, looking out over his slaves powering away his clock tower.

Looking left to right, up and down, Emmy saw several cave openings on the other side of the clearing. The mouth of these caves opened directly next to the clock tower. Emmy knew in that moment they needed to find a way to get over to that side of the clearing without crossing the middle and being seen by the Watcher. They needed to find an entrance to the cave, so that they could exit out by the clock tower. How to get to the entrance, she did not know.

"We need to get over to the other side of the cave," Emmy said, pointing over to the opposite side of the cave where the mouths of two smallish corridor openings were gripping her attention.

Jack, now squinting but keenly laying his eyes on the mouths of the two corridors on the other side of the clearing, took his turn. "I see it!"

Scanning the area some more, Jack spotted a tunnel underneath where the Watcher loomed a high distance away up on his ledge. "Underneath the Watcher, over there!" Jack had an idea. There was a small tunnel opening underneath where the Watcher resided high up on the ledge. "If we can make it over to the wall right over there, underneath the Watcher, we can head into that tunnel. There might be a way through there to exit back out by the corridors near the clock tower."

It wasn't much, but it was something. Emmy and Jack both communicated this to each other with a simple look, no words necessary.

"For Sam," Emmy said.

With a brief moment's hesitation, Emmy and Jack again found themselves gazing longingly into each other's eyes. The pair of best friends, missing their third counterpart, found something warm there. If not for the urgency at hand, and the safety of their best friend Sam, they would have preferred to stay lost in that moment forever. Unluckily for them, a large clock tower and a monstrous, evil being lurked just beyond the comfort of their veil of shadows on the wall. They needed to move.

Breaking the silence, Emmy spoke out. "Don't get all gooey on me, dingus." Emmy grabbed the hand of Jack, who was still lost in the moment, and the pair continued their trek along the wall.

20

Arriving at their destination, Emmy and Jack quickly realized that this tunnel seemed different than the others, more intimate. Light from torches lined the walls, sconces emanating flames as soon as they entered. They also hadn't realized when eyeing it from the other side of the clearing, but this tunnel was massive. Way bigger than any cave they had been in up to that point. Its sheer circumference left them baffled. The only thing they could think of was that it was fit for a large being. It was fit for the Watcher.

"At least we can see in here," Emmy said.

"Yeah, it's also warm and toasty," Jack responded. "I like warm and toasty."

This comment made Emmy chuckle and feel good, a feeling she wished stayed longer than it did.

"Do you think Sam is one of those zombie kids?" Emmy asked.

"He has to be. And if he is, that means there's still hope," Jack responded.

"But what if he's stuck like that? What if they all are stuck like that?"

The thought struck instant fear into their hearts, a dagger coming down swiftly and with great force.

"We'll find a way, Emmy. I know we will." Jack spoke softly.

"I know we will, too," Emmy said, with a half-smile.

The oversize tunnel gave way to a new grand hall. Approaching in slow steps, Emmy saw the gigantic throne of clocks before Jack did.

"What the heck is that?" Emmy yelled.

"Shhhh, quiet, Emmy. We need to keep . . . *ert dwern* . . ." Emmy grabbed Jack's chin with a tight pull, smushing his lips together and twisting his head in the direction of the throne of clocks. "WOW! Look at that thing!" Jack, freeing himself from Emmy's hand, screamed, clearly forgetting about his request for quiet just moments before.

The throne of clocks really was an incredible sight. Yes, Emmy and Jack had borne witness to some sensational and quite unbelievable things since arriving down through the peculiar tree, but this was magnificent.

Emmy and Jack ran up to the throne to get a better look.

Emmy eyed the throne up, down, and all over, taking in its massive appeal. The size of it wasn't the only thing that grabbed her; the clocks themselves were magnificent. They were all so different and unique. Emmy thought back to the pink and purple, sparkly, butterfly-winged clock she had seen earlier.

"This must be where he sits," Jack said.

"Ya think, dingus?" Emmy responded sarcastically, as only she knew how.

Running her hand over all the different clocks that lined the throne, Emmy stopped when her hand reached a green clock breathing in and out, more so than all the others.

This one is fresh.

Emmy picked up the green clock and pulled it away from the throne, like a magnet coming off a fridge. "Jack, look at this!"

Emmy turned the clock around and saw exactly what she now expected, a white shamrock.

"What is it, Em?" Jack said.

"Recognize this?" Emmy asked.

"Hey, that kinda looks like Sam's lucky shirt," Jack said excitedly.

"Bingo, Jack. It was his name-o," Emmy said.

"This is too bizarre." Jack whimpered.

"Maybe not," Emmy said with a tone of renewed hope. "Do you remember what Sam said?"

"Sam said a lot of things, Emmy."

"No, last night." Emmy realized that she didn't know exactly what time it was, so last night might not have been the best choice of words. "At our sleepover, what he said about the Watcher."

Jack thought for a moment, trying to remember the distinct details of what Sam had said. He remembered Sam telling him and Emmy the legend of the Watcher, but he couldn't recall the specifics.

"Sam said that the Watcher watches all the children in the world. He watches them at all times. Do you remember, now?" Emmy needed Jack to remember.

And he did. It came flooding back to him in a pool of remembrance. "YES!" Jack called out. "He said the Watcher has a clock for every kid in the world!" Realizing now where Emmy was going with this, he spoke again. "This is Sam's clock."

In her hand, Sam's clock, a mirrored image of his lucky shirt pulsed in and out.

21

The Watcher looked out over his work, a smile of sheer bliss spreading over his face. He watched his three new monsters retreat back and out of the cave, off to do his evil bidding. He knew that with the power of the witch twins Gramilda and Bramilda, as well as his three new monsters, soon he would have enough power to rise from his underground trap. He would once again head to the surface and rule the Earth he once called home.

The Watcher knew his time was coming; he felt the raw power shift in his veins. His powers had been growing for centuries, and now they were radiating exponentially. One by one, the children piled up as slaves for his clock tower. Each one's life force another notch on his belt. Each one giving his powers a small boost.

Although the Watcher knew his time was near, he also knew his work was not yet complete. He had to bide his time just a little while longer. Just a few more children. In the grand scheme of things, what was a few more children, anyway? He knew how close he was; he sensed it. The power rushing through him was tantalizing his senses. His growing powers told him everything he needed to know.

A sly grin on his face, the Watcher turned away from the ledge that stood looming over his clock tower and began his retreat back to his throne, where he would wait for his minions to bring him the souls of more children. *Only a matter of time now.*

Of course, this particular time, walking back over to his throne was different than all the others. Different than the thousands upon thousands of times he had made this walk before. The Watcher's underground cavern may have been full of milky, pale, lifeless children and all kinds of creepy monsters, but it was mostly a lonely place. Just the way the Watcher liked it. This time, when the Watcher made the similar walk back over to his throne of clocks, he was not alone. There, as he sauntered over, were two ugly little children. Even worse, they were holding one of his clocks.

22

"I think we should get out of here," Emmy said. "I don't want to stay in this cave too long. Something tells me it's not a safe place to be."

Emmy and Jack found out quickly that Emmy was exactly correct. The Watcher's underground cave was extremely dangerous, as evidenced by the disgusting monsters that dwelled in every nook and cranny, but the heart of the cave near the Watcher's throne, where they resided at the moment, was perhaps the most dangerous.

A massive roar interrupted Emmy and Jack before they even had a chance to notice the Watcher creeping up from behind them.

"AHHHHHHHHHHHH!!" A piercing shriek of terror escaped Emmy's lips. She was frozen in her tracks, still barefoot and all, as the roar ripped her attention over to where the Watcher had entered their vicinity.

Jack saw the Watcher and knew he had to think and

act quickly. That was near impossible, given the incredible volumes coming from the Watcher's roar and Emmy's shriek. It felt like the two were having a karaoke competition, and whoever could sing the loudest and the longest would win.

Finally ending his destructive roar, the Watcher lifted a long digit from his gargantuan arm and sent a rip of dark green lightning directly at where Emmy was standing.

Finally able to think clearly now that the Watcher's roar was done, Jack grabbed Emmy's right hand (her left still clutching Sam's clock) and pulled her in toward his body. The lightning missed her by a few inches. The force of pulling her in toppled them both over, and Emmy landed on top of Jack.

Once again, the two found themselves staring into each other's wide eyes. No time to enjoy or not enjoy the moment, Emmy and Jack both looked over in unity at Sam's clock in Emmy's hand, then again in unity back over to the Watcher, who seemed to be prepping for another flash of lightning.

They both uttered the word at the same exact time: "RUN!"

In one motion, two surfers popping up on their surfboards, ready to shred some gnarly waves, Emmy and Jack leaped off the ground and pumped their legs as fast as they could. They heard another crack of lightning from just behind them as they exited the clearing where the Watcher's throne of clocks sat.

They pumped until they were out of sight from the

Watcher. They knew he would be hot on their trail, but they figured his one weakness was that he wasn't as fast as they were in these caves. The Watcher might have the upper hand in speed if it were a big field, or a straight shot, but his massive frame probably made it difficult to navigate these caves as quickly as they could. They also had the advantage in that moment of being quite a bit smaller. Although the Watcher's size and strength was a nightmare, Emmy and Jack were tiny and could hide in the shadows, if the opportunity presented itself.

Pumping their legs, attempting to get as far out of reach from the Watcher as possible, Emmy and Jack knew they had no choice but to go find Sam, and fast. They had been found, outed. The Watcher knew they were there, and he would be hot on their heels. Their barefoot heels.

Panting, Emmy called to Jack, "We need to find Sam!"

Following the tunnel, they ran as fast as they could. As far as they could see, the Watcher was not following nor right behind them. They also knew this would not be the case for long. They had to move fast.

Finally making their way out of the tunnel, they instantly took in the breadth of the large clock tower from up close and personal. It was massive. Their plan had worked. Exiting out of the tunnel, they found themselves directly in front of the large structure.

"He has to be here," Jack said, taking a long look at all the children working the clock tower.

"He's here, all right. He has to be! But where do we even begin?"

The magnitude of the dire circumstances they found themselves in weighed considerably. Emmy and Jack needed to find Sam, and they needed to find him now. It wouldn't be long before the Watcher discovered their whereabouts once again. Once that happened, they were no match for him. They, too, would become lifeless and ghost-white beings, doomed to power up the Watcher's clock tower forever.

The only rational plan either could think of given the gigantic size of the clock tower was to just walk its circumference. It was a plan with little to no hope, but they knew they had to try something. They had come so far in such a short amount of time. *Was it a short amount of time?* Again, time became a lost memory to Emmy and Jack while they were down in the evil caverns of the mangled tree. *Has it been hours? Days? Weeks? . . . Years?* How much time had passed since they had gone down there, they had no idea. What they did know was that rules up above did not apply down there. Not in the slightest.

Emmy and Jack took one step closer to the clock tower, standing only a few feet from it now. Seeing the soulless children up close and personal was terrifying.

"I don't want to end up like this, Jack." Emmy trembled.

"We won't! I promise. I will never let the Watcher get you. Now let's find Sam and get out of here!"

Grabbing Emmy's hand, Jack and Emmy started

running furiously around the clock tower, keeping a close watch on all the empty kids.

One by one, they passed them by. Child after child, they looked on in terror. The scariest thing was that none acknowledged Emmy and Jack's presence, made eye contact or even looked up from their levers for a second. Emmy thought, *How could the Watcher do this?*

"There are too many kids," Emmy said. "We'll never find him!"

"We have to keep trying, keep looking, Emmy!" Jack, sounding exasperated, exhausted, and feeling hopeless, replied.

In that moment of dread, already feeling like there was no chance of success, the Watcher emerged from another large tunnel not far from where they were standing. Even worse, directly opposite him, surrounding them on both sides with no chance to escape, was Bramilda the witch.

"FOOOOLLSSSS!!!" the Watcher roared. "HOOOWWW DAAREEE YOUUU ENTERRRR MYYY LAIIRRRRR!"

In all of his years reigning terror, no one who wasn't one of his minions had ever stepped foot inside of his underground cave. The dead tree was a stronghold entrance. No one without magical powers was able to enter, this the Watcher was sure of. So how did they manage to defy the odds? By chance, of course. But also friendship and the strongest of wills to save their best friend. "GEETTT THEMMMMM!!"

Bramilda the witch heard the command and let out a

cackle of heinous, high-pitched laughter, as only she could.

"He he he he he he. It would be my delight, master," Bramilda said, smiling, her blue skin radiating a heavy, piercing glow.

Bramilda inhaled a long breath of air, as wind started to form in the cavern. The wind circled up into a small, cyclone-like circle, turning dark blue with tiny shreds of electricity beaming from within. Bramilda let out the breath of air, and a vile smell erupted along with the circling wind.

"I think I'm gonna barf," Jack said as the smell stung his nostrils, temporarily paralyzing him.

Luckily, Emmy did not get the brunt of the pungent odor. It had hit her but not terribly. It was rotting eggs and sewage, that she knew.

Seeing the electric-blue cyclone rapidly making its way over to them, this time Emmy grabbed Jack's hand, brought him in close, and leaped out of the way, the cyclone passing them by and dissipating back into the arid air of the cavern. Lying on the cold floor, their backs hard against it, Emmy and Jack looked on as they had a renewed sense of hope. Staring back at them, a knight in shining armor, was the peculiar creature Emmy had named Stony.

Stony launched himself into the air, a firework exploding up into the sky. With renewed force, it clomped down onto Emmy's hand, shattering Sam's clock into shredded pieces.

23

Sam, startled, woke from his catatonic daze. He looked around and took in his surroundings. He had been slightly conscious in his zombie like stupor, just unable to act on any impulse. The Watcher had stolen his soul, his life force. He was cold, dark and empty.

But now the feeling of life, of happiness, exploding back into him, Sam awoke anew at his post. He immediately stopped grinding the lever staring him directly in the face and tried to figure out how this had happened. Somehow, some way, he was saved.

Sam took a long, healthy look at the clock tower and children all around him. He noticed that all the other children were still zombielike. He was the only one to have awoken, come to his senses. Although the feeling of existential dread had been lifted, Sam knew that his window to escape was now. He needed to make a move and get out while he still could. He would send help, though. Sam promised himself in that moment that if he did make it out of the Watcher's icy death grip alive, he would come back for the rest of the slaves here and put an end to the Watcher's evil.

Although Sam's arms and legs felt asleep, pins and needles, still waking up like the rest of him, he took several anxious steps away from his post at the clock tower.

It only took Sam a brief moment to see but what felt like a lifetime to comprehend: There, standing a mere fifty feet away, were his two best friends, Emmy and Jack.

24

"Hey, Stony! What'd you do that for!?" Jack yelled at the seemingly unapologetic rock.

Jack's attention was quickly halted at the sound of his best friend's, Sam's, voice.

"Emmy! Jack!" Sam called out with every ounce of noise his tiny lungs could handle. It came out a screechy squeak.

"SAM!!" Emmy and Jack both shouted in unison.

Sam ran at top speed, his legs now feeling awake and as alive as ever. The three friends reached one another and indulged in the tightest group hug. They stayed that way for several seconds, embracing the incredible moment. A reunion of epic proportions.

Tears streaming down her face, Emmy spoke. "I missed you, Sam. Don't you ever leave us again, ever!"

"It's good to have you back, dude." Jack spoke with his chest held high, proud of the bravery he had exhibited on their journey, but also accepting the incredible accomplishment it was seeing Sam in the flesh again.

Sam let out a half smile, not allowing a full celebration until they were out of this nightmare cave. "Best friends for life," he said, releasing his hug on Emmy and Jack. "Now, let's get out of here before we're Watcher meat!"

"Well, isn't that cute! He he he he he," Bramilda the evil witch said. "It's a shame that all *three* of you will be ours now! He he he he he." Bramilda's evil laugh echoed in the cave.

Bramilda reared back again, breathing in the dry air of the underground cavern, gearing up to exhale a smelly, pungent cloud and turbulent, blue cyclone. Before she could finish, though, Stony interrupted her.

"Shoo, shoo, he he he." Bramilda kicked at Stony, who was rolling around in circles by her feet, bouncing on her massive, disgusting toes. "Leave me be, foul thing! I'll grind you to dust!"

Bramilda went to grab Stony off the ground, but he was too quick for her. She missed pretty handily. Stony evaded her attempt and rolled to her other side.

Bramilda turned around and tried again, this time lunging her arms all the way to the ground. But again, Stony quickly rolled away from this attack and spun in a circle around her.

Growing increasingly frustrated, the clumsy witch started grabbing frantically at the ground in hopes to wrangle Stony. On he went, rolling around, allowing Bramilda no real chance to grasp him, confusing her in every which direction.

Bramilda had circled around so many times trying to grab Stony, she now stood up on her heels and wobbled. Stony knew he had won; the battle was over. She was dizzying back and forth, so Stony made his final move. He launched himself into the air and clomped down onto Bramilda's head, most certainly leaving a mark, and down she went. Bramilda fell back on her humongous behind, into her own dream world.

"ENNNOOUGHHHH!!" The Watcher's voice startled Emmy, Sam, and Jack.

The Watcher slowly rose his arms, and in them green lightning radiated back and forth. The Watcher was preparing a massive offering of power to throw directly at them.

Not wanting to wait to find out, Stony hopped up and down repeatedly, doing his best to communicate the message to Emmy, Sam, and Jack.

"Follow Stony! Go!" Emmy called out.

"How do you know to follow him?" Sam said.

"I just do, trust me. Now, go!" Emmy clapped back, pushing Jack and Sam forward and in the direction of Stony, who was rolling away at top speed.

Looking back over her shoulder, Emmy saw the giant, green, radiant bolt of energy explode behind them by the mouth of the clock tower.

25

"This way," Emmy said, taking on the role of tour guide, leading the way behind Stony. On and on, he rolled through the vast caves and tunnels. Stony rolled at a swift pace, knowing their exit needed to be quick.

Emmy, Jack, and Sam followed as fast as they could, all three drained in their own ways.

"So what was it like?" Jack said.

"Dark," Sam responded. "Dark, cold, and scary. It felt like all the happiness was pulled from my life. And even worse, it felt like it would never return."

Emmy sniffled at Sam's words. "Well, you're back, now. And you're never going anywhere ever again."

Sam wanted to believe Emmy was right, but the sheer memory of being back at the clock tower, all good things sucked away into the darkest depths of the Watcher's lair, had shaken him. He felt his brow bead with moisture and the hair on the back of his neck rise.

"And then all of a sudden, it was like a breath of fresh air, and all the feelings came rushing back in an instant. I could feel myself again. My thoughts, my feelings, my movements. All my senses alive again," Sam said.

Emmy's attention was pulled back to Stony, at the front of the line, who was jumping up and down with excitement. "Look!" Emmy said. "The entrance to the cave!"

Sam and Jack stared just a few feet ahead where the cave opened up into the mass gathering of tunnels where they had originally entered.

"This is incredible!" Sam said, taking in the magnificent scene in front of him.

"Oh yeah, sure! It's great," Jack spoke sarcastically. "Just be glad you didn't see the jelly monster."

"Jelly monster?"

"We have a lot to talk about," Emmy, laughing heartily, said.

Emmy examined the floors surrounding all the cave exits. "There!" She pointed over to the trail of shoelaces she had left. "Don't you love it when a plan comes together?"

Emmy, Jack, Sam, and Stony, the unorthodox group, continued their escape, heading on over to the cavern where they had come in.

Sliding along the darkness of the walls, they realized there was one major problem with their escape.

Jack smoothed his hand along the far end of the wall, remembering the entrance being open when they came in. "This is definitely where we came in. It has to be." Jack sounded exasperated.

"There has to be a way to open it," Emmy responded, looking all around the cave's walls for something to pull. A button to push, anything.

Emmy's gaze was interrupted once again by a large thrumming coming from the mouth of the cave. "Quick, hide!"

Emmy, Jack, and Sam all rushed into the dark side of the cave wall. Stony rolled behind them and ducked into darkness. They painfully pushed their backs against the wall.

The cavern panel rose to the thrumming noise. After it was open wide enough, Gramilda, the grotesque, wretched, green-skinned hag, poured in, prancing along on her giant, fat feet. Behind her, she dragged a seemingly hopeless young boy.

"Off to the depths we go, now you are ours, young boy, to see the Watcher you must, and forever you'll be my toy! He he he he he." Gramilda cackled in delight, dragging the poor thing along.

Keeping as still as possible, Emmy had closed her eyes in fright. She peeked one open when she knew Gramilda was almost out of sight. Staring back at her with glossy eyes, the young boy pleaded for help silently.

26

Back on the surface, Mill Falls was vibrant and alive. Nightfall had drawn on the small town, and the spirit of Halloween was in full swing.

Jack-o'-lanterns littered the lawns of town folk everywhere the eye could see. Decorations of monsters, zombies, ghouls, and witches festered in every nook and cranny; above and below; on houses, trees, sidewalks, and lawns. Everywhere in town was decorated. Oranges, purples, and greens lit the darkness of town well.

Children dressed in spooky, extravagant costumes and were running amok all over, bouncing from house to house with giant bags of candy by their sides. Small children with bags half their size! One particular kid's bag was bursting from filling it with too much candy. It was clear the stitching on it was not going to hold much longer.

Witches, pumpkins, skeletons, and the like ran around with gleaming smiles, knocking on doors, saying "trick-or-treat!" and being greeted by the nice parents of the town. Of course, the parents of Mill Falls were always swept away by the Halloween spirit and gave out the best candy. Giant candy bars were the minimum in this town.

"Hey, let's go to that house!" a young boy dressed as a T. rex said, flopping his inflatable tail around.

"I'm so tired, can we just call it a night?" The T. rex's sister, dressed as a ballerina, responded. "It's almost nine. Do you remember what Mom said?"

"Yes, of course. Be home by nine. I remember."

"So then, that's a no!" the ballerina said.

"Oh, come on. PLEASE. Last house, I promise," the T. rex pleaded, looking up at the big house. "They have to give the best candy, look at the size of this place!"

"You know how much I hate you, right?" the ballerina said to her Jurassic brother.

"Thank you, thank you, thank you!" The T. rex wobbled his big, inflatable frame over to his sister and gave her a big hug with his tiny, little clawed arms.

Running in unison, the T. rex and ballerina headed over to the massive house before them. It was truly an incredible sight: a massive white mansion with a green light careening down its front surface, making it look almost as if an alien spaceship was beaming down on it from above. Its shutters were spray-painted orange with evil pumpkin faces stickered onto them. Cobwebs hung down over most of the front of the house, with incredibly large plastic spiders attached to them. On the front stoop, lawn, and walkway, dozens of spooky Halloween decorations festered. Right by the front door, a monstrous wolfman decoration loomed, ready to attack any trick-or-treaters. Not far from the wolfman, over to the left side of the house, was a vampire baring its fangs, showcasing a tiny drop of red blood. Moving out onto the grassy lawn, several glowing headstones made up a small graveyard. *Here lies Amanda Masterson, 1625–1676*, one stone said. A skeletal hand protruded up from the grass in front of the glowing headstone. And finally, jack-o'-lanterns with various razor-sharp grins and jagged eye holes looked out from the lawn.

Ding-dong. The doorbell chimed out in the incredible house they arrived at, but there was no response.

"Ring it again," the T. rex said.

Ding-dong. Once again, the doorbell chime rung out through the large mansion. Still no response.

"All right, they're not home, Billy," the ballerina said to the T. rex. "Can we please go home, now?"

"No, not yet! Ring it one more time!" Billy yelled to his sister.

"Last time! And then we're going home."

Billy's sister, the ballerina, lifted her finger and lunged it toward the button, preparing to ring the doorbell again, but before she even pressed it, she was greeted with a creaking noise. The door slowly opened.

There was light inside the house, but it was dim. Billy looked at Ashley, his sister, and gulped.

"Hello?" Billy called out. "Anyone home?"

In the house, Billy and Ashley couldn't see much. The only thing visible under the dim lighting was a smallish wooden table on top of a multicolored rug that sat below an old chandelier.

"Helloooo?" Billy called again.

"Come on, Billy. Let's just go home. There's clearly no one here."

Immediately after she finished her sentence, Ashley was met with a loud, thunderous roar and a scream. Something rushed out of the darkness and leaped out at her.

"RAAHHHHH!" The creature snarled, terrifying Ashley and Billy.

The T. rex and ballerina went storming back down the front steps, over the grave of Amanda Masterson, and on, engulfed by the darkness of Mill Falls.

"Ha ha ha ha. YESSSS," the creature's voice called out from the front stoop of the large mansion. More giggles could be heard in the background. "That was so unbelievably excellent."

The creature that had ripped out from the darkness took off the ghoul mask he was wearing, stepped back inside of the mansion, and shut the front door.

"You're so evil," Max Harrison said from the couch in the living room to his best friend, Ronnie Tarp. "You could have just given the poor kids some candy."

"Well, *where's* the fun in that, huh?" Ronnie responded, his hair a sweaty mess from the mask he had on.

Max and Ronnie were two of the most popular

eighth graders at Mill Falls Middle School. Their parents were out at a Halloween party that night, as was tradition. They were left on candy duty.

Most of the parents in town usually gathered on the scary night at the town hall for a big Halloween bash. It was mostly an excuse for them to get away from their boring lives.

"All right, let's get back to it," Ronnie said shutting off the lights once again and pressing play on the Blu-ray player.

The score of John Carpenter's *Halloween* hit, and the two jocks were entrenched back into the 1978 classic.

It wasn't long after they had started the movie that the doorbell chimed once again.

"Don't these kids know that it's getting late? The time for trick-or-treating is over. Can we please just enjoy our movie?" Ronnie said. But then a sly grin slowly appeared on his face. He looked over at the ghoul mask.

"Oh, you are evil," Max said.

Ronnie quickly re-shut the lights, put on the ghoul mask, and headed toward the door.

Ding-dong. Ding-dong. Ding-dong. Ding-dong.

The doorbell kept ringing on repeat. Ronnie let out a light chuckle. He knew this would again be excellent. These trick-or-treaters, judging by the way they were ringing the doorbell, just like the rest of 'em, were anxious to get to his house. They always were.

Ronnie went on with his routine, slowly creaking open the door, and then when the time was right, seconds later, he jumped out!

"RAHHHHH!!!!" Ronnie stood there baffled though, as nothing happened. This was normally the part where the trick-or-treaters ran screaming. Their reactions were his favorite.

"This is the part where you run away screaming," Ronnie said.

The trick-or-treaters simply stood there, staring back at him. There was no reaction, nor was there a response of any kind.

"Hey, those costumes are pretty neat," Ronnie said, taking off his mask. Again, his hair was in a sweaty flop.

A pumpkin, mummy, and troll stared at him, long-eyed and again with no response.

"All right, well you guys go on then, and have yourselves a nice Halloween. Here, take a candy bar." Ronnie lifted the purple candy bucket off the ground near the door. He grabbed several bars and went to hand one to each before realizing there was nothing for him to put them in. No sacks, no bags, no buckets.

"All right, I'm closing the door now," Ronnie said.

What a buncha weirdos. The door wouldn't budge, though. Ronnie gave it a harder push, but the door was stuck, frozen in place.

The pumpkin lifted up a long, stalky finger at Ronnie. An orange glow shot out from it and fired directly at him. The light immediately swallowed him, twisting Ronnie up into a light-speed force of orange glow, rotating thousands of miles per minute. The spinning light continued for no more than five seconds before Ronnie was transformed into a large pumpkin seed.

Looking down at his work, the evil pumpkin let out a sinister cackle. He lifted the seed up off the ground and put it into a small green pouch he kept by his side.

"Ronnie? Everything okay?" Max called from the living room. It wasn't long before he was greeted by the Watcher's three evil henchmen.

27

Sam, Emmy, Jack, and Stony emerged from the decrepit old tree right where they had entered. Although nighttime had come and it was harder to see, Emmy recognized it instantly.

"Man, am I glad to be out of that place," Jack said.

"You're telling me!" Sam spoke, a renewed sense of belonging in his voice.

Emmy hesitated before responding. She looked down at Stony, an artifact from their adventurous travels down the tree of time. "Yeah, I guess."

"Something wrong, Em?" Sam said.

"What about all those kids?" Emmy answered. "We need to help them!"

Sam and Jack looked at each other, knowing she was right.

"First, we need to go home," Sam said. "My parents are probably worried sick right now. I wouldn't be shocked if there were a town-wide search party for me. For all of us."

"No. We can't," Emmy said emphatically.

"Are you kidding, Emmy?" Jack responded.

"Not at all, none of us are going home to our parents. If we do that, then the whole operation is done. They'll never believe us and put us on house arrest. We won't be able to leave or go anywhere."

"Em, listen to yourself. What are you actually saying? Our parents are worried sick, and we need to go home," Sam said.

"You can go home," Emmy responded. "I'm not going anywhere until I help all those kids." She looked down at Stony. "Even if this rock is all that I have."

There was a moment of silence between the three best friends. Stony stood as still as a stone—a normal, nonliving stone.

"Em, you don't know what it was like." Sam's cheeks puffed up and grew red as he spoke. "I still feel it. Deep inside of me. I know he's not here, but there's a part of him with me now, and I'm not sure if I can ever get rid of it." The hairs on Sam's nape stood up, frozen in fear. Sam looked away from Emmy, almost embarrassed by his words.

Emmy walked up to Sam and wrapped him tight in a big hug. "Which is exactly why we need to rescue the rest of those kids. I'm frightened, too. I'm scared of my own shadow, for crying out loud. But something down there changed me. Seeing the faces on all those kids. Seeing your face, Sam, changed me. We need to do something. I don't want to lose you again," she said.

Jack joined in their friendly embrace.

Loosening his embrace, staring at his two best friends, his saviors, the reason why he was no longer in the muddy confines of the Watcher's underground lair and icy grip of doom, Sam spoke. "I'm in. What's the plan?"

"Jack?" Emmy said.

"I'm in, too. But this time, I'll be ready for that jelly monster," Jack said with a smirk.

"Stony?"

All three friends looked down at the rough-surfaced stone that hung down by their feet. Stony jumped up and down twice, showcasing his glee at their motion.

"Okay, so we'll need to get supplies. That's first. We can't go back down there without being prepared," Emmy said.

"Okay, but how do we get to one of our houses without being seen?" Jack spoke up.

"Oh, well that seems easy," Sam's face lit up with enthusiasm. "It's Halloween, durr! We need to find ourselves some costumes."

All three best friends nodded in approval. The first part of their plan was in motion.

Sam, Emmy, Jack, and Stony peaked out from the side wall overlooking Harry's Halloween Mishaps and Mayhem, the local ma-and-pa Halloween store that had been in town for as long as they could remember. Harry and Maude's shop had been around since 1973 and served the great town of Mill Falls well.

The odd grouping of kids and stone peered out, trying to get a good look in the windows of the shop. They had to get in there without being seen. It looked as though they might still be open, but of that they could not be sure.

The group inched out and sidled along the wall, heading up to the side-wall window to get a better look inside. There wasn't anyone around, it seemed. The coast was clear on the outside.

"Scoot over, dingus!" Emmy nudged Jack over a smidgen.

"No, you scoot over, Em! I can't see because your nasty breath is fogging up the window!" Sam spoke.

"Yeah, Emmy. Don't you know what mouthwash is?" Jack said, giggling.

Sam took a step back from the window, as Emmy was locked in. Her hands cupped over her face, trying to peak in as best she could, ignoring her peripherals. Jack was the only one to notice Sam's several-step retreat.

Sam did his best not to laugh but motioned for Jack to "shhh" as he took another step back. He gave notice to Stony, who also didn't seem too keen on the idea but ultimately obliged.

"Guys, I don't think anyone's in there, I think they are closed for—" Emmy didn't have a chance to finish before Sam snatched her from behind, reminding her of how much of a scaredy-cat she was.

"RAHHHHH!" Sam shook her, startling her away from the window of the Halloween store.

Jack and Sam let out low chuckles, careful not to be too loud. Even Stony rolled back and forth, seeming to enjoy the first moment of genuine laughter in quite some time.

Emmy humphed and angled Sam off of her. She blew up and away from her eyes a strand of her cherry-blonde hair that had fallen down.

Hands on her hips, smile forming on her lips, Emmy crept up closely, and the tickle fingers came out. They quickly engulfed Sam all over. He begged for her to stop.

"Okay, okay. Let's get it together, people." Jack spoke as the voice of reason. "We need to keep it down. We're trying to save the world, remember?"

All three friends again peered in through the window, and finally there was movement. Both Harry and Maude had crept out from a backroom and stood by the cash register. They were crunching numbers and holding receipts.

"It looks like they are closing out the day. We have to be careful," Emmy said. "Let's make a move."

Luckily, the front door was still open, and all three friends entered in one fell motion. A bell chimed, signaling the arrival of someone new.

"I'm sorry, but we're closed for the night," Harry Campbell called out to the chiming bell.

The three kids and Stony silently creeped into a side

aisle, careful not to be seen or heard.

Excruciatingly slowly, Harry stood up from his creaky wooden stool by the cash register and gazed to the front of the store. Customers trying to get last-minute costumes or masks weren't anything new to Harry; he had seen it all over the years.

"Now, like I said, we're closed." Harry was just able to see the glassy front door from his angle, but there was nothing there. He lifted his toes and shifted side to side to see just a little bit more, but the shop appeared empty.

Harry crept out to the center station of the store, but footsteps and skittered movement captured his attention. He jerked his head over to where the noise came from, but there was nothing but a wolfman mask that dangled on its hook.

Then he heard the skitters from behind him. He jerked around and looked for anything, any sign of the intruder. Yes, Harry Campbell had owned and operated his Halloween store for over forty-five years, but this was the first time he had ever actually felt scared. He wanted to call over to Maude to phone the police, but he convinced himself he knew better.

Damn kids.

The bell chimed again, and with as quick of a pace as his old legs would allow, Harry Campbell rushed over to the front door. All that was left were footprints made of dirt from what seemed like bare feet, and a slim trail of grass stain that seemed to have rolled right on through the store.

28

"FOOOLLLSSS!!!" the Watcher yelled angrily from his throne of clocks. He stared down at the bumbling twin witch sisters.

"Sorry." Gramilda and Bramilda spoke in unison, their heads held low. Bramilda was holding her pointy hat in her hands. Her thin and wispy black hair matted to her head.

"NUUMMMBSKULLSSSS!"

"Sorry."

"BUFFFOOOONSSS!"

"Sorry." Bramilda put her hat back on and looked up for a brief moment at her enraged master. His facial expression snapped at her, immediately forcing her head back down in fright.

"HOOOWWW could you let this happen!?" The Watcher looked away in pure disgust. "Defeated by KIDS, nonetheless. MERE CHILDREN! Not when I'm so close! It's taken me centuries to get back the energy and power that I need to rise once again. I am almost there. I can feel it. I will NOT allow the insufferable stupidity of you two to jeopardize my hard work!"

"But, master, it wasn't just the three twerps! They had help from the rock, master." Gramilda was scared to look the Watcher directly in his eyes, so she kept her gaze down at the ground while she spoke.

"Ahhh. Yess. The stone. Don't think I've forgotten about that one. He will suffer for his betrayal. Once a child, that very stone yielded to my powers. I made him a slave before, a minion to work my tower. He will pay for his act of disservice. THEYY ALLL WILLL PAYYY." The Watcher's words were louder than ever, rattling his underground lair, several clocks tinking down to the ground.

"Of course you will, master. You are the great and powerful Watcher!" Gramilda said.

"Yes, your time is still here, master!" Bramilda followed up. "Do not let these three insolents ruin anything. Our time is close, master!"

"SIILLENCEEE," the Watcher roared, a hiss of smoke exiting out of his elongated snout. The Watcher curled his obscenely long-fingernailed digits into a closed fist. A half smile spread across his scaly face. "Yeesss, this is correct. My powers are on the verge of exploding. I can feel it—I'm almost able to return to my rightful place up above. The time to rise from the filth of this dirty cave is now. Go, witches. Do my evil bidding and bring me those kids. BRING ME THEM ALIVE!"

29

"Check out this haul!" Sam said.

"So, are we technically criminals now?" Emmy clapped back. "Because I don't want to be a criminal."

"I think these are extenuating circumstances, Em," Sam replied. "I'm pretty sure the police would have to understand that we're trying to save the world. It might even be a law."

"It's not a law, you dingus," Emmy said.

Jack pulled his findings out from their bag and reveled at the ghost costume he had picked off the rack. He really wanted to be a Ghostbuster, but their time was short, so he had to choose quickly back in the shop. For a ghost costume, it was pretty neat. The sheet that acted as the ghost's long, formed body was made of super soft, cottony fabric. And the eyeholes where he would look out from were two large, black deformed patches. It wasn't like a standard bed-sheet ghost costume. It was actually kind of spooky.

"Hey, you look great!" Sam said, gazing at Jack who had fully costumed up. "That's an awesome costume!"

"Yeah, maybe for a dingus," Emmy said, pulling down at the tattered bottom of Jack's costume.

"Beee CAAArreeffull, EmmYYYY, orrr the GhhOOOOsstt of Jackk will HAAAunntt youuuu forrrEEEEVVVERRRR." Jack spoke with long vowels and oohs and aahs for added effect, wrapping his sheeted arms around Emmy.

Sam, tending to his own bagged costume, whipped his head around at his two friends goofing off, and he hissed with his bloody fangs. "Silence! Your insolence will no longer be tolerated. I'm afraid the time to feed is now, and I vant to sack yur BLAD!" Sam took two steps over to Emmy and motioned to drain her neck, as a creature of the night.

They all giggled together. Stony rocked back and forth, joining in on the fun.

"What'd you get, Em?" Sam said, relinquishing his vampiric grip on Emmy, allowing her to pull out her costume.

Putting on her fairy wings and sprinkling a sparkle of fairy dust at her two friends, she mouthed the words, "Bless you."

Jack and Sam grabbed their chests, as if the magic spell from the fairy had killed them. A painful death for their evil souls at the hands of the good fairy. They fell to the ground.

The ghost, vampire, fairy, and rock made their way through the darkest of Halloween nights. They blended right into the Halloween spirit that surrounded them. Even if there was a search party for them, about which they still had no idea, they were completely in costume, and it was doubtful anybody, even their parents, could recognize them. This was, of course, the goal. If they were going to get themselves ready to head back down to the Watcher's secret, underground cavern and put an end to his reign of terror, they needed to do so in secrecy. If they were found, if anybody had recognized them, it was possible their whole operation would be put in jeopardy.

"Can we at least do some trick-or-treating before we try to save the world?" Jack said, his words slightly muffled through the ghost costume's sheet barrier.

"No, we can't go trick-or-treating, dingus," Emmy said.

"Come on. Just a few houses. I'm starving!" Jack begged.

"Jack, you know we can't do that. Not only do we need to act fast, but we can't risk getting caught." Sam spoke as the voice of reason.

"He's right," Emmy replied. "The Watcher knows we're here, he knows that we escaped, and he knows that we stopped him once. He's probably lurking down on his throne of clocks right now, coming up with all the different ways to capture us again. Whether we like it or not, we have to finish this. And we have to finish this tonight."

30

Gramilda and Bramilda, the evil but clumsy twin witch sisters, rose to the surface, their goal to heed the Watcher's directions closely. They were to find and capture those three vile children who had escaped from the Watcher's underground cavern and return them to their destiny of becoming one of his lifeless minions, working the clock tower forever.

"All Hallows' Eve," Gramilda, the grotesque, green-skinned witch, said, seeing the costumes of the children of Mill Falls all around her. "What a marrrvvveelloousss night."

"These children are gross no matter what, and in costumes they might be, bring them back to the Watcher we must, and forever they'll never be free, he he he he he." Bramilda, the shiny, blue-skinned witch. replied to her sister, taking in her surroundings.

"Hey, you're ugly!" A small boy wearing an oversize skeleton mask over his head stopped right in front of the witch twins. His blond hair was poking out the back of his mask, his candy sack bulging, and his blue eyes pierced at the witch sisters.

"He he he he." Bramilda laughed. "Did you hear

what he called you, Grimmy?"

A slow, sly grin spread across Gramilda's face. "Oh, Brimmy. I think I did. How so very kind of you, young boy. I take that as the highest compliment, my child." Gramilda the witch panned her face and leered mere inches from the boy's face. "Now say it again, little boy. I dare you."

The young boy was hit with a smell so foul, he was forced to take his mask off, to alleviate the stench from his nostrils. "You stinky, fat, ugly witch!" the young boy said, coughing into his fist.

Her smile spread even wider now, Gramilda lifted her face ever so slightly from the boy's and turned to look at her blue sister. The two witches nodded in approval at each other before they both aimed their attention back to the boy.

Each lifting one hand and pointing a finger at the boy, both witches began their chant:

"UP ABOVE, YOUR TIME HAS COME,
SAY GOODBYE TO MOMMY AND COME DOWN TO OUR CAVE,
OUR HORRORS AWAIT YOU, BE VERY AFRAID,
UNDERNEATH THE WATCHER AWAITS,
TO MAKE YOU HIS SLAVE!"

The boy felt a tingling sensation pinch his body, first starting with his stomach, and then spiraling out toward his toes, fingers, and then slowly making its way to the rest of his body. In just a few moments, the tingling subsided, and the boy yelled up at the witches, at first not realizing what had happened.

"Hey, you're even weirder than I thought," the young boy called out. He started to take one step away before a monstrous creature skidded in front of him several feet. The boy jumped back in fear before realizing it wasn't a monster at all, it was just a cat. The biggest cat he had ever seen.

"Be careful, boy, that cat looks hungry, he he he he he." The two witch sisters cackled with delight.

The boy looked back at the witches, who he now noticed were gargantuan giants. "Hey, what did you do to me!?"

Gramilda lifted the tiny boy, who was now no more than the size of a peapod, and carefully placed him into the pocket of her raggedy cloak, gleeful as she did so.

"Hey, let me out of here!" The boy wiggled in her pocket, and his voice came out muffled.

"Pipe down, little one," Gramilda said, patting at her pocket. "If you keep it down, we'll not feed you to the cat, he he he he!"

Gramilda and Bramilda went off into the night, in search of three best friends and a rock.

31

The trio of besties and their rock counterpart looked out from a tiny bush on the far side of Sam's front lawn.

"Hey, my aunt Judy!" Sam said, glancing into the front window.

Mrs. Strong and her sister, Aunt Judy, sat at the kitchen table with hot mugs in their hands. Mr. Strong stood by his glassy-eyed wife's side, rubbing her shoulders. In just the next room over, a police officer was looking at a big dresser, rubbing his finger on the top of it and taking notes.

"Poor mom," Sam said again. "I wish I could just tell them I'm okay, that everything's going to be fine."

"Is everything alright, Sam?" Jack said.

"I guess not," Sam replied hesitatingly.

Stony sensed how upset Sam was. Although there wasn't much for him to do, he nuzzled next to Sam to show he cared.

"Everything *is* going to be okay," Emmy said to Sam,

Jack, and Stony. "I know it will. I don't know how, and I don't know how long it's going to take, but I know everything's going to be okay."

"How do you know that, Emmy?" Sam said.

"Yeah, what about the witches? The jelly monster? The clock tower?" Jack said, frightened.

"Because we have one another," Emmy said.

Her words must have struck a chord because Jack was silent, and Sam wiped the one tear that had formed around the corner of his right eye.

"Now, we need to get out of here and find supplies! We can't go to Sam's, we'll be seen." Emmy had just finished her sentence when several cars zoomed up the driveway of the Strong household.

"Mom and Dad!" Jack said in a low whisper, careful not to be heard by his parents.

"Mommy!" Emmy followed up Jack's cries to his parents with her own.

The two cars belonged to none other than Jack's and Emmy's parents, who parked and immediately went inside, hugged the Strongs, and joined them at the kitchen table.

Stony looked on sadly. Although his tears could not be seen, there was something about all the parents together that made him emotional. He retreated a few rolls. Emmy noticed this and made a mental note of it.

"This is perfect!" Emmy said.

"On what planet is this perfect?" Sam replied.

"All of our parents are in there right now crying

because they think we're missing," Jack said.

"Well, technically we still are missing."

"They'll be fine," Emmy said. "The point is that if all of our parents are here, then no one is at Jack's house or my house."

Jack, Sam, and Stony now understood what she was saying and nodded.

"But we have to go now," Emmy said as Jack and Sam followed her, scurrying away into the night.

Emmy only made it a few steps before noticing that Stony wasn't following. She looked over and realized Stony was still peering into the Strong household. Something in there kept his attention.

"You coming?" Emmy said to the rock.

Stony wasted no time. He brought his attention back to the group, a renewed sense of vigor in his roll, and he scurried on past Emmy.

32

Sam, Emmy, Jack, and Stony arrived at Emmy's mom's house. Emmy's dad had left them many years ago, when she was still in first grade. She thought about him occasionally but to her, it was his loss. She loved her mom, and that's what was important.

"Your mom really slacked on the Halloween decorations, huh, Em?" Jack said, looking at the severely lackluster decorations on the house. It was mostly bare except for one jack-o'-lantern on her front stoop that seemed to be missing a mouth. There were two eye holes but nothing else.

"Yeah, as if you could do a better job, dingus," Emmy clapped back.

"She could have at least made a mouth on the pumpkin." Jack bent down to examine the jack-o'-lantern.

"At least she put out candy," Sam said, realizing in that moment just how hungry he was. It had been hours and hours since he had last ate. Bending down to grab a sweet treat from the green bucket labeled *Take only one, please*, Sam noticed there was nothing left. "Or not," he said, turning the bucket upside down to show his disapproval to his friends.

Emmy picked up the rug on the front stoop and examined underneath for a key, but nothing was there. She looked around to the adjacent areas and in the nearby bushes, but the key was nowhere to be found.

"She always leaves the key here, but I guess she was nervous and must have put it away. You know, with me being missing and all," Emmy said.

"Good thinking, Emmy's mom," Sam said.

Getting an idea, Emmy walked over to the side of the two-story house where her small bedroom window was. "Mom doesn't know, but I always keep this window unlocked. Fingers crossed," Emmy's crew followed up behind her.

She put her fingertips under the lip of the windowpane, looked over at her friends with a *Here goes nothing*-type half smile, and pulled up.

Much to her surprise, the window lifted with relative ease. "Jackpot!" Emmy lifted one leg up and over the windowsill and onto the desk in her room, doing her best not to let the wings of her fairy costume get caught. One by one, her friends followed her in. After Stony hopped over the gap in the window, landing with a loud knock and making a dent in her wooden desk, Emmy closed the window behind them.

Jack and Sam went right through Emmy's room and on to the kitchen, where they found the giant bag of candy Emmy's mother seemingly forgot to put out.

"Right on, Ms. Wheatley!" Jack called out, shredding wrappers and stuffing his mouth with candy.

"Looks like somebody forgot to put out candy!" Sam replied. He, too, went on unwrapping handfuls of mini chocolates and opening candy boxes.

Emmy saw the two bozos pigging out on her left side in the kitchen, but on her right, her attention was focused on the refrigerator door. Her gaze was focused on a picture-frame magnet stuck on it. It was a picture of her and Mom, smiling ear to ear. Emmy Wheatley and her mom were basically identical twins. Both short with cherry-blonde hair and smiles that lasted for days. Emmy shared the same two trademark buckteeth in the front of her mouth. Emmy pulled the magnet off and held it down in front of her.

Thinking deeply of her mom, Emmy was caught off guard when Stony nuzzled up next to her, around the pantleg of her fairy costume. She also had completely forgot that she was barefoot up until that moment.

Emmy reminded herself that Stony had a similar reaction in Sam's driveway when her mom and Jack's parents had arrived. He had stared in the window, at their parents sitting at the kitchen table, for quite some time.

"What is it, Stony?" Talking to a rock had become somewhat normal for her at that point. Once the jelly monster rose up from the dredges of the dirt-filled cave, she knew any and all things were possible.

Stony nuzzled her pantleg one more time before

jumping up and lightly tapping the magnet Emmy was holding.

"Do you like this photo?" Emmy said.

Again, Stony jumped up and tapped the magnet, careful not to tap too hard.

A thought came to Emmy. "Let's try this." Emmy got down on one knee to be more level with Stony. "You seem to be smart and understand what I'm saying, so I'm going to ask you some questions. If the answer is yes, I want you to hop once. If the answer is no, I want you to hop twice. Got it?"

Stony hopped once, seemingly excited about this new form of communication.

"Okay, great!" Emmy also approved of their new system. "Next question."

Stony rolled back and forth in excitement.

"Do you like this picture?"

Stony hopped once, indicating that yes, he indeed liked it as he had previously conveyed to her.

"Do you like that I'm in it?"

One hop from Stony.

"Do you like that my mom is in it?"

One hop from Stony.

"Do you like that we're at the park in the picture?"

Stony hopped twice this time, indicating that he didn't care much for that aspect of the picture.

"Do you like that Sam and Jack are pigging out on candy right now?"

Two hops from Stony, indicating he did not care

about that, either.

Emmy thought for a moment, trying to come up with another question that might help her deduce what Stony was thinking. It came to her.

"Do you like that my mom and I are in this picture together?"

Stony not only hopped once this time but rolled in circles. Emmy knew she had hit the right chord.

"Did you like seeing our parents together at Sam's house?"

Again, Stony hopped and rolled around, showing his excitement.

"Do you like that they were sitting at a table?"

Two hops from Stony. The table did not matter.

"Do you like that they were drinking coffee?"

Two hops from Stony, and he came down strikingly hard the second time, showing Emmy she was getting colder with her questions.

"Okay, okay calm down. I got it." But before she had a chance to answer another question, Stony zoomed over to the back door of Emmy's house, rolling into it several times.

Emmy followed him while the two dinguses were belching and guzzling some soda. "Do you want to go outside?"

One hop from Stony.

Emmy opened the door and followed Stony out into the grassy backyard. Stony began furiously rolling in the grass, back and forth, in circles making all kinds of motion.

"What are you doing, Stony?" Emmy called out to him, but the rock did not respond. He just went on, rapidly attacking the grass.

"What's going on out here?" Sam and Jack exited the back door and made their way outside.

Emmy stood, closely watching Stony work, without acknowledging her friends walking outside.

Several moments later, Stony's movement had subsided, and he carefully rolled over to Emmy, nuzzling her pantleg.

The three friends walked closer to the grassy area and noticed what the rock had boldly done. There, etched out in the grassy backyard, in dirt letters, were the following words:

Miss my family

33

Gramilda and Bramilda, the evil witch twins, made their way through the small town of Mill Falls. They traversed the sweeping waves of costumed children flooding the streets and sidewalks. To the townsfolk, they were just a couple of old gals out on the town, basking in the fun of the Halloween spirit. In reality, they were two evil baddies with the most heinous goal in mind. They were in search of three young children whom the town police had not officially started a search party for and a silly little rock that they wanted to crush like dust.

"Ohh, Brimmyyyy," Gramilda said, as the witch twins arrived at a sidestreet called Inverness Drive.

"Hmmmmm, sister?" Bramilda replied.

Gramilda lifted her pointy, wrinkled, and warty noise into the air and sucked in a long sniff. Pointing a razor finger over to a bare house with no decorations, she said, "What do we have over here, he he he he?"

Bramilda then followed her sister's routine, breathing

in a long sniff, searching for the scent whose trail they were hot on. "Smells like bratty children who need to be taught a lesson, he he he he."

The two witch sisters cackled in unison before trekking up to the bare house with only a small but empty candy bucket on the front stoop.

34

"We have to help him," Sam said, staring at the dirt letters glaring back at him.

"So let me get this straight," Jack said. "Stony has a family? Like, a rock family?"

"No, you dingus. Like a real family." Stony jumped up and down at Emmy's mention of his family.

"But, he's a rock," Jack replied. "Just a rock."

"He's just a rock . . . now," Sam said convincingly. Jack and Emmy hushed at his words. "What if he wasn't always a rock?"

Stony slowly rolled up to Sam, appearing to look up at him from invisible puppy-dog eyes.

Sam bent down and spoke to Stony, forming a new connection with the rock. "You were down there, weren't you? Just like me. You worked that clock tower for too long, and this is what happened to you."

As bashful as a rock could look, Stony did. He slowly rolled around in a circle, a kid wandering aimlessly, looking down at his feet.

"Don't worry, Stony. We're going to help you. We're going to defeat that evil Watcher and save all the children he enslaved down there. We'll figure out a way to transform you back, promise."

Stony nuzzled his pantleg, showing approval for the plan.

"Talking rocks that used to be living children. This just gets better and better!" Jack said. "If we're going to do this, we need to do this right. We need supplies."

Emmy, Sam, and Stony nodded in approval, and the group sauntered back inside to prepare for their adventure back down into the wondrous, evil caverns where the Watcher dwelled.

"What are you doing, dingus?" Emmy called out to Jack, who was making a mess with a large jar of peanut butter and some bread.

"What? I'm making us sandwiches. We could get hungry down there," Jack said.

"Jack, we need supplies, not food," Emmy said.

"Food is supplies, Emmy. We don't know how long we may be down there. I'm just making sure we have nourishment," Jack replied.

Emmy, hand on her hip, stared at Jack without saying a word.

"Fine, then. You can't have any of my delicious

peanut butter sandwiches. Stony can have yours."

Emmy couldn't help but giggle, looking down at the rock. Thinking about Stony eating a peanut butter sandwich was just so foreign and hilarious to her in that moment. "Do you even eat, Stony?"

Stony hopped twice, indicating he didn't need to eat.

In the other room, Sam was filling a bag with all kinds of stuff he thought they needed: a phone charger, compass, notebook, binoculars, batteries, plastic baggies, Band-Aids, hat, bug spray, and a slingshot. He then grabbed a lighter off of the mantle, where Emmy's mom kept it to light an occasional candle and put it in his pocket. Last, Sam walked over to the screen door where he saw a baseball bat. He picked it up and motioned a practice swing. "Try and evade that, monsters." Which of these items they would need, he did not know. What he did know was that anything was possible down in that underground cave, and he needed to be as ready as ever.

Sam reentered the kitchen where Jack was wrapping sandwiches in tin foil and Emmy was lacing up her sneakers super tight.

"Put these in your bag," Jack said, handing the sandwiches to Sam.

"Oh, wait!" Emmy had a light bulb moment, remembering something important.

Jack, Sam, and Stony looked on as Emmy ran in her fairy costume and trainers to the living room. She started rapidly opening cabinet doors, frantically looking for something. "Got it!" Emmy exclaimed.

Jack and Sam exchanged a confused glance.

Emmy ran back into the kitchen with a bounce in her step. "Shoelaces!" Emmy said. "Breadcrumbs, so that we can trace our way back through the cave." Emmy held in her hands massive amounts of various-colored shoelaces. Emmy always thought her mom was a little cuckoo for keeping such a large amount on hand. *But Mom was always right*, she thought.

Sam, Emmy, Jack, and Stony stood in a small semicircle in the kitchen of 17 Inverness Drive, the residence of Emmy Wheatley. They were garbed in full-blown Halloween costumes, which they had to steal from Harry's Halloween Mishaps and Mayhem, much to their chagrin. They had internally promised themselves that they would make it right by Harry and Maude when the time came.

Emmy lifted a winged arm and put it in the middle of the semicircle. "There's no turning back now."

"We're ready," Jack replied, putting his hand in the middle.

"For Stony." Sam finished the act by putting his free hand over the hands of his two friends. The other wielded his baseball bat.

"For all the kids in Mill Falls, all the kids in the world, all the kids whom that stupid monster is always watching. At all times," Emmy said, and Stony hopped up and rested himself on the hands of the three friends, showing that he, too, was in.

The group burst into a small fit of laughter, but it was quickly interrupted by a loud bang coming from upstairs.

35

"Did you guys hear that? Emmy said.

"It came from upstairs." Jack motioned over to the side of the kitchen, where the staircase leading upstairs resided.

"Jack, don't go. I'm scared," Emmy said.

"Oh hush, Emmy. It was just the wind." Jack walked up the first two stairs. *What if it wasn't just the wind?*

Sam rushed over to the staircase to accompany Jack, baseball bat in hand. "I'm not letting you go alone, dude," he said.

"You guys are really freaking out over nothing. I got this," Jack said, stumbling on the bottoms of his ghost costume up the stairs.

"You sure about that, dingus?" Emmy called him out for tripping.

Jack fixed himself, pulling up the dredges of his ghost costume, and peered out of the two black-patch eye holes up at the top of the staircase. Jack had been in the Watcher's underground cave of nightmares. He had seen the horrors down there. He walked on bravely to the next step because nothing could be worse than that. Or so he thought.

Jack only made it halfway up the staircase, Sam several steps behind him, when a huge crackle of green light exploded half the staircase, sending Jack sprawling backward into Sam's arms and down to the bottom step.

"Good evening, brats, he he he he he!" Gramilda, the wrinkly green-skinned hag, spoke. A fresh glint in her eyes, as she lifted a broom she undoubtedly had found in the upstairs closet. Gramilda hovered into the air and darted down the staircase toward Jack and Sam. "The Watcher will see you now!"

Thinking quickly, Sam and Jack, fully decked out in their vampire and ghost Halloween costumes, rolled to their left, back into the kitchen, to avoid the ugly witch.

"Did you miss us, he he he he he?" another voice sounded, entering from the living room into the kitchen. Bramilda, the shiny blue-skinned twin, greeted them from the other end of the kitchen, striking intense fear into all of their hearts.

Sam tried to stave them off by swinging the baseball bat in their direction.

"What do we do?" Emmy said, Stony by her side, joining her two friends who were backpedaling away on the floor of the kitchen.

"We need to run!" Sam said, as memories of being a slave in the cave of nightmares came rushing back to his senses, a jolt of fear exploding into his mind and body. The hairs all over his arms and nape immediately stood straight up, and he broke out into a sweat.

Inching back a few more feet, the trio with their rocky companion stood up in a swift motion and jolted toward the side entrance of Emmy's house. "GO! GO! GO!"

The group high-pedaled it over to the door, knowing that one false step could mean they would be enslaved by the Watcher for eternity. Of course, Jack's and Emmy's legs were long warmed up at that point from all the running they had previously done. On they went.

"Not so fast, he he he," Gramilda said, hovering several feet in the air from a raggedy old broomstick. "Come with us, back to your home, to work the tower, and waste you to the bone!" Gramilda said, sending a wave of green energy at Stony.

The wave of energy was a direct hit and lifted Stony into the air, sending him swirling in a stream of green light directly back into the hand of Gramilda. The glow of the green light wrapped Stony in some kind of funky forcefield where he couldn't move.

Gramilda took a long look at Stony. "Welcome back, child," Gramilda said. "My how we missed you, too, he he he he he." Gramilda placed Stony into the patchy satchel she had at her side.

"NOOOOOO!!" Emmy called back, a well forming in her eyes.

"STONNYYY!!" Sam called out as well.

Jack, who felt the same way, tried to reason with his friends. "Come on! We need to go!" Jack pushed his two friends out the door and into the blackest of Halloween nights in the small town of Mill Falls.

36

"Whoa, whoa, whoa, well, what do we have here?" Johnny Harrison, former king of Mill Falls Middle School, but now just a freshman aspiring to be prom king one day, spoke as three pretty well-costumed children approached.

"Yeah, who dressed you goons? Did Mommy and Daddy get you those costumes?" Johnny's best friend, Dave Carlson, said.

Johnny was the leader of the group, but Dave was his right-hand man. Although they were freshmen, the writing was on the wall. They were already mostly in with all the popular seniors of Mill Falls High School. It was only a matter of time before they ran the school.

Johnny slicked back his shiny blond hair and popped out the collar on his leather jacket. Johnny was too cool to be dressing up for Halloween, now that he was a ninth grader. He was decked out in all black, though. He had a pumpkin pin on the top right of his leather jacket.

Dave dressed similar to Johnny, though he didn't quite fill out his leather jacket like Johnny could. He was still on the thin side, but he didn't mind because he knew the ninth-grade girls, even some of the tenth-grade girls, loved it. Dave was still on the smaller side, while Johnny had a bigger, more muscular build.

Johnny and Dave stood up from the stoop they were crouched on. They were flanked by several of their groupies, as they approached the pumpkin, mummy, and troll.

"Hey, I'm talking to you," Dave Carlson said, a strand of his jet-black hair falling over his eyes."

There was an odd warmth coming from the pumpkin, troll, and mummy. Dave felt it radiating almost immediately when he approached them up close. What it was, he didn't know, but he started to think something might be off.

"He said he was talking to you!" Johnny Harrison, acting as leader of the pack, backed up his friend's threat and shoved the troll, to no avail.

The troll's feet didn't budge in the slightest. His eyes never wavered from the group of ninth graders, either.

"Ew, gross. What the heck, dude?" Johnny's hand was covered in a thick, green snot that must have covered the troll. At a closer look, Johnny realized it was. The troll was completely covered in disgusting green snot.

Johnny tried to wipe his hand on his jeans, but the snot was way too thick. He wasn't sure it would ever come off.

The troll methodically pulled out a petite ax he had hidden in his side pocket and held it up toward Johnny Harrison, whose blond hair had completely fallen down to his sides. Sweat was beading down his forehead.

"Hey, it's cool, man. We don't want any trouble," Johnny said at the sight of the ax. Behind him, Johnny could hear his groupies scurry away. Dave stayed, though. *Dave is a good friend*, he thought. One day they would run Mill Falls High School together. Just the two of them.

The snotty troll lifted the ax at waist length, and a green crackle of energy emitted from its tip and out toward Johnny.

"Hey, stop! What are you—" Before Johnny had a chance to finish his sentence, he was engulfed in a large green beam of light, his senses dulling and a wet slickness forming all around him.

The change only took seconds for Johnny but it took Dave Carlson a lifetime to comprehend. He looked over at where his best friend Johnny was standing just moments ago. Now, in his place, was a giant booger, about a foot wide and a foot tall. It almost looked like a giant green egg covered in snot.

Dave looked up at the troll who had since lowered his ax and was now giggling like a hyena along with his two costumed freaks.

Frightened to his core, Dave spoke. "I-I-I-I d-d-don't know what's happening here, but this is messed up. You guys are dead."

Dave began to back up slowly, keeping his eyes on the trio of monsters, when the mummy speedily shot out a white wrapping from his hand. A whitish light quickly came over Dave, and he pleaded for help as he was morphed into a small, round, egglike ball completely covered in mummy wrapping.

"Run!" Several trick-or-treaters from the next house over noticed what had happened to the two boys and cried out, fleeing in every which direction. Candy flailed from all over as trick-or-treaters frantically tried to race away. Various forms of costumes popped off and fell to the ground in the frantic chaos.

When the dust settled and the area was dull and quiet once again, nothing was visible except for the three evil monsters. The troll, mummy, and pumpkin all looked at one another and laughed, a heinous and sinister chuckle.

37

"Master, master!" Gramilda hissed her tongue out from beneath her two fat, crinkly lips. Her sister trailed right behind her, grinning ear to ear. The witch twins knew they had done well.

"Look what we brought you master," Bramilda said.

But before they even made it to their boss, who was sitting, watching his giant throne of clocks, Gramilda clumsily tripped over her own feet. On her way down, the patchy satchel she kept at her side, now holding precious cargo, launched out from her wide hip and fell several feet in front of her toward the Watcher.

The satchel was patched up and closed using magic, so the squirming coming from within brought the witch twins nothing but joy. Stony wobbled all around the satchel, trying to burst free, leaping up and down within the confines of the sack, doing his best to escape. His efforts were met with failure.

Picking herself back up, dusting off dirt and grime from her fat belly, Gramilda picked up the satchel that held Stony and presented it to the Watcher.

"What do you say, master?"

The Watcher remained seated. He had plenty on his mind, but he knew that his witch twins, his top-two henchwomen, had done well almost immediately. They were clumsy, that he knew. But they had proven themselves to be almost as evil as he and that, he knew he could count on. The Watcher lifted the satchel, felt the rock poking side to side, squirming and looking for any way to get out.

"Excceelllennnttt," the Watcher said, rattling the caves of his main cavern. "You've done well, my witches."

"Oooohhhhhh," Gramilda and Bramilda said in unison, hopping up and down in delight, clapping their hands together.

"But what about the children?" the Watcher roared.

Gramilda and Bramilda shot a worried glance at each other before smiling excitedly and responding. "That's the best part, master," Bramilda said.

"Yes, that's the best part!" Gramilda replied.

"That's what I just said, Grimmy!"

"No, that's what I said, Brimmy!" Gramilda said. "Now, the children have no choice..."

"The children have no choice, master," Bramilda interrupted her sister, hopping up and down in excitement.

"Will you shut up, sister?" Gramilda scolded her annoying twin, patting the side of her raggedy cloak.

"Sorry, Grimmy," Bramilda replied.

"The children have no choice, master . . . because now that we have the rock . . ." Before she could finish her thought, Gramilda was once again interrupted by her fumbling sister.

"The children have to come back and rescue it, he he he he!" Bramilda, unable to hold in her thoughts, yelled out.

"Bramilda, will you STOP INTERRUPT—" This time, it was not Bramilda interrupting her but the heinous bellow of their all-powerful master, the Watcher.

"SILENCE!" the Watcher said.

Gramilda and Bramilda patted and smacked each other back and forth, two siblings fighting over control of the TV remote.

"You two idiots cannot even have a conversation without fighting and interrupting!"

"Sorry, master," Gramilda said.

"Yes, sorry master," Bramilda followed.

"Now, your allegiance to me is unwavering, and you have proven once again you are MOST EVIL, HA HA HA HA HA!" The Watcher's vibrating words echoed throughout the cave. "Those three disgusting, foul children have no choice but to come rescue their silly little rock. Once they do, we will be ready for them."

Gramilda and Bramilda, the evilest twin witch sisters, scurried off back into the cave of nightmares, skittering about clumsily, clapping together in unison, for now they would await the arrival of Sam, Emmy, and Jack.

"But in the meantime, I think it's time to have some fun." The Watcher spoke to himself, gaining his composure and rearing his massive claws for a display of power. He rose his gnarly, humongous arms into the air, chanting a low hum. No words or understandable language, simply a deep and sinister thrum from his throat.

Up above, his powers would soon be felt, and that brought a rather large smile across the Watcher's face.

38

"Oh man, this is bad," Jack said.

"We have to get Stony back," Emmy replied.

"Everyone stay calm. We need to keep it together," Sam said, hands on his hips, huffing and out of breath.

Sam, Emmy, and Jack had run so far and so fast that they didn't actually recognize where they were at first. Their chaotic flight from the evil twin witch sisters left them broken and confused.

"What are we going to do?" Emmy, also out of breath, looked to her two best friends for guidance. "We can't let those monsters win. We have to go after them and get Stony back. We have to do something. We have to—"

"Emmy!" Jack gripped Emmy by her shoulders, standing directly in front of her and ripping off his ghost costume. The two locked eyes as they had done previously, when they were alone in the cave of nightmares. "We are going to rescue Stony. We are going to rescue all of those kids and end that evil monster's reign of terror. But we need to keep our cool. And we need to do it together. We need you right now. I . . . need you right now."

A wave of calm came over Emmy almost immediately. She took a deep breath in before squeezing Jack to her so tightly, she thought she may have been hurting him. She didn't care.

Sam looked on at his two best friends, a tear forming in his eye. He thought about joining their hug, but he wanted to give the two their moment. He realized then that there might be something more there than just friendship. That made him smile.

Jack and Emmy released their grip on each other and gained their composure, retreating back to a three-person squad. By themselves, they could be defeated. All together, they knew they could do anything.

"Emmy is right," Sam said. "We need to act fast. The Watcher's powers are on the cusp of exploding. Once he has enough children and power to rise back to the surface, it won't matter what we do."

"So we need to go back to the cave of nightmares, and we need to go now," Jack said, putting back on his ghost costume, as he saw trick-or-treaters in his peripherals.

"Okay, but only one problem," Emmy said. "Where are we?"

The trio looked around, realizing then that they needed to find their way back to the tree of terror before doing anything else.

Looking around, Sam thought the area seemed

familiar but also new and different. "Isn't that Kenny Northrup's house? He lives in my neighborhood," Sam said, realizing they weren't very far from his home.

Looking up at the sky, Jack saw massive black clouds. They cast an eerie, more-than-evil glow on the entire street. Small flashes of green lightning began to form all over, snapping away like an endless popping of bubble-gum bubbles.

Then Jack and Emmy realized that they, too, knew where they were. Everything looked different, though. Everything was spooky. The trees all around them seemed to have died and rotted, looking more like the trees of nightmares. The grass was turning purple and withered. A bushel of buttercups over by the Northrup residence had completely blackened and died.

Just then, a hand, grotesque and skeletal, shot up from the blackened and purple lawn of the Northrup residence and sliced the soil in two. Up it shot like a rose creeping from the root, but this was not a rose. This was something sinister and evil.

The skeletal hand grew into a skull, and then an empty chest cavity, before finally emerging fully from the ground. Just a few feet away, another skeletal hand rocketed out from the soil. Up it rose, making its way to the surface until the entire skeleton had found its way up.

"Um, this is not good. I repeat. This is *not good!*" Jack said.

More and more of the skeletons began creeping up from the ground and running on their bony skeletal legs. They ran awkwardly and slowly, legs skittering out weirdly side to side, but they kept growing in numbers. In just a minute, a dozen more of them had risen up from the ground.

The trio of friends looked on as two of the skeletons made their way over to a small group of trick-or-treaters at a nearby house. Each of the skeletons grabbed a trick-or-treater from behind, clenching them in a tightly wrapped hug. There were four trick-or-treaters in total, and the two that were unwrapped let out bloodcurdling screams, running away in terror.

The two unfortunate children trapped in the confines of the skeleton hugs began to slowly transform. With each passing second of the skeletons' hold, they were morphing, shrinking down into tiny skeletal figures of themselves. When the act was complete, the skeletons stood holding their new prizes, the miniscule skeleton figures of the children. The skeletons creaked their heads up the road in the direction of another group of trick-or-treaters. They trotted on slowly, and it wasn't long before Sam, Emmy, and Jack heard more ear-twisting screams.

"RUN!" Jack yelled, and the trio of besties hightailed it out and away from the horrors of the neighborhood.

Passing through other houses, other developments, they quickly realized the horrors had engulfed more than just one development. Skeletons seemed to be running amok everywhere, holding tiny skeletal children in their hands. Parents were flailing their arms about at their sides. "Donnie! Donnie!" one parent called out to their child, as he was whisked away by a nearby skeleton.

Sam, Emmy, and Jack ran as fast as they could without looking back on the horrors that befell their quaint little town of Mill Falls. They kept moving without communicating with one another in the slightest. Emmy was in front because she was the fastest, and her two friends followed her lead.

It wasn't until they made it all the way to a quiet, isolated spot near Sam's house that the silence was broken.

Emmy, ducking behind a bush, took a peek through Sam's front window, where previously their parents had been sitting at the kitchen table with hot beverages. "They have to be out looking for us," she said, breathing in and out heavily, hunched over hands on her knees. One of her fairy wings was slightly bent down at an awkward angle.

"All the lights are off inside, but the cars are still here," Sam said.

"Which means they are probably out on the streets somewhere, and it won't be long before they see what we just saw," Jack said.

"We can save them." Sam looked up at his two besties as he spoke, brimming with confidence.

Jack wiped a huge, glossy layer of sweat and grime off his forehead with the bottom of his ghost costume, which was now not as white as it was an hour ago. He tuned in and listened to Sam.

Emmy's labored breathing had subsided, and she also listened in closely.

"We can save them all," Sam said again. "If we defeat the Watcher, we can save all the children of Mill Falls and the world."

"But how do you know? This mission could be a death sentence! Did you see those skeletons? How do you expect us to beat him, now?"

"And we're going to his house, his cave; he has home-field advantage. I have a feeling that we only saw a brief glimpse of the horrors down there," Emmy said.

"Because I was one of them," Sam said. "And you saved me. Do you remember that?" Sam was asking a rhetorical question. "Didn't that seem like an impossible task?"

Emmy and Jack both glanced at each other with faces that said Jack was correct.

"And now we need to save the rest of them. If we defeat the Watcher, the rest of the children will turn back to normal. I know it. Just like I did."

"But we didn't have to defeat the watcher to save you," Jack spoke out.

"No, it was the clock!" Emmy replied.

"Exactly," Sam said. "Stony destroyed my clock. The Watcher keeps a clock for all of us down in that horrible place. He *watches* us while we're kids because once we're older, he has no power over us. That's why all of his slaves are kids. He's watching our time, carefully waiting for the perfect time to strike on us all."

Jack and Emmy listened on as Jack made perfect sense. Horrible and nightmarish but perfect sense.

"The souls of the children, he keeps down there to give him his power. He sucks the souls out of them and stores them in the clocks he has for each until he's ready to use the souls in his clock tower."

"And that's where his power comes from," Emmy said.

"The clock tower," Jack responded.

"If we destroy the clock tower, we destroy the Watcher," Sam said.

"We save the children," Emmy smiled.

"We save everyone," Jack said.

Although their plan was easier said than done, they knew what they had to do. The fairy, vampire, and ghost kept their cool and trudged on, heading back to the evilest of places.

The trek back to the tree of horrors was rather easy. They traced back the steps they had followed earlier that morning, which seemed an eternity ago. The three walked with a melancholy demeanor, few words being spoken. The excitement of their plan had been rejuvenating and fresh for them, but the thought of acting it out had shaken them. They knew this was still a long shot, no matter how they sliced it. They had barely made it out alive the first time.

"There it is!" Jack spoke through his ghost costume. He ran up ahead; after all, it was he who had followed the witch's ugly footprints earlier and originally stumbled onto the tree.

Emmy and Sam followed closely behind, arriving at the withered, old, and lonely tree.

"He's waiting for us," Sam said, staring at the wide-open mouth of the cave entrance.

"He kept the tree open for us," Emmy looked at it cautiously.

Sam, Emmy, and Jack turned to one another one last time before stepping foot inside. The three had formed a semicircle, holding hands. "Whatever happens, you guys will always be my best friends," Sam said.

"For life," Jack replied.

"No other dinguses in the world I'd want to head down into this nightmare with," Emmy called out.

And with that, the three best friends, still completely garbed in their Halloween costumes, took their first steps back inside the Watcher's underground cave of terror.

39

The Watcher could sense their arrival. He knew they were close. His plan was working swimmingly, and he loved when a good plan came together. "Pippeee downnn, rock!" the Watcher called out at the small satchel in his hand.

Stony was making soft, squeaking noises and bouncing up, down, and side to side in the satchel.

The Watcher lifted the satchel up to his eye level to speak to him. "How does it feel, little one? How does it feel to be back in my icy grip of doom, HA HA HA HA?"

Stony knew there was no point. He ended his frantic movements. Any hopes he had of rescue lay in the hands of the three brave and curious kids he had befriended. But he was still excited. He worried for the children's lives, as he didn't want the same fate that had befallen him to take them. But he had been down there so long, and this was it. If there were ever a moment for him to muster enough mental capacity to remember what life was like before this nightmare, to have a glimmer of hope, it was in that very moment, curiously enough, while he was knotted tightly inside of the Watcher's satchel.

The Watcher held the satchel with the tightest grip and called to his evilest henchwomen. "Gramilda! Bramilda! Comeee hereeee, my clumsyyyy but evil minions."

"Oh, master, thank you, thank you, he he he! You are too kind!" Gramilda said, scurrying over to him, flopping her big, fat feet up and down.

"Where is that disgusting, bulbous, and most wretched sister of yours?" the Watcher said.

Before Gramilda could respond, her shiny, blue-skinned twin pranced over, mumbling something that sounded like a greeting, but it was impossible to tell through the large, fat beetle that protruded from her mouth.

"They are close," the Watcher said. "I feel them upon us. They are entering now; it won't be long before they are within our domain. I think we should greet them the best way we know how, yes?"

Bramilda slurped up the remains of the juicy-morseled bug she was eating and looked at her twin sister. The two smiled at each other, knowing exactly what the master was referring to.

"He he he he he he." They both cackled in unison, scurrying off back through the chamber.

The Watcher, most pleased with his henchwomen, again raised the satchel to his eye level. "Do you remember, little one? Do you remember that wondrous day, young master William?"

Hearing his real name, the tiny rock thing now referred to as Stony worked hard, searching deep down into whatever memories he had left. And then, it came to him.

40

William Clark, exhausted from the most fun day at the carnival with his ma and pa, sat down on his favorite, creaky wooden chair. He pulled the eroded candle closer to him, preparing to read by candlelight.

"William, don't you think it's time for bed?" William's ma said to him.

"Oh, not yet, Ma! I just want to stay up a little bit longer to read my book. Please, Ma?"

"William, you know you have to be up early for football with your friends in the park," William's pa said.

William hated football. He played, and he was actually pretty good, so the confidence booster was nice. But he hated it. William's pa, though, was always wanting him to play. "Be a man, William!" he would say. "Football is for real men like us Clarks!" he would say. That was all well and good, William knew. Football was a fine game, and he cared deeply for his friends who played. It just simply wasn't his thing. William would rather read a book or write in his journal. He loved stories, and he loved to write.

"I know, Pa. I'll be up, I promise!"

Pa gave William a scowl before ultimately succumbing to his request. "Fine, fine boy. But make sure you keep it down and get to bed soon. You *will* be playing football tomorrow. I've got a petty wager with Joseph Smith's pa that the boys will pick you as captain tomorrow. I know you won't let me down."

"Right on, Pa." He hugged his father lovingly but also reluctantly. William knew his father wanted the best for him and just wanted him to fit in with the rest of the boys. For that, he was grateful. "Love you, Ma." William turned to his mother and embraced her tightly.

"You heard what your father said." Ma returned his hug with one of her own.

As soon as the door to their bedroom closed, William raced back to his favorite, creaky chair. It was a gift from his uncle John for his tenth birthday a few years ago. Uncle John was a master craftsman. The hinges were loosening slightly from incredible amounts of use, but the chair still held up exceptionally well. William pulled his candle closer to his chair and scooped up his book from the side table. William was reading *The Scarlet Letter* by Nathaniel Hawthorne. William loved to read all kinds of books and write his own stories in his notebook. He was very much enjoying *The Scarlet Letter*, as it gave him an idea for his own story he wanted to write. If only he knew that he would never get to finish it.

William was rocking back and forth calmly, taking in his book, when the voice called out to him.

"Wiiilllllliaammmmmm."

He looked up from his book and over to the staircase, but there was nothing. *I must have imagined it*, he thought, and he went back to his reading.

Moments later, the voice called again. "Wiiillliammmmmm."

William was certain he heard something this time, and it was not simply his imagination.

He picked up his candle and walked over to the staircase. "Ma?" he whispered, careful not to wake her if it wasn't indeed his ma who called to him. "Pa?" William again whispered his call to his pa. He could already see the look his father would give him for waking him up. He could forget about staying up late to read if that was the case.

Still, William could not find the root of the voice calling to him. *Must be the wind*, he thought.

William sat down once more in Uncle John's chair and was about to pick up his book when he heard the voice again, and now there was no doubt in his mind that it was real.

"Comeee play with meeee, William," the voice hissed.

William shot from his chair and ran over to the window. He opened the shades, chipping a small part of wood in the process. Looking out into the darkness of night, William saw nothing. He opened the window and heard the screams of the wind. William poked out his head and called to the voice. "Is there anyone out there? Are you in need of assistance?"

"Yess, Williammmm. I needd your help, boyyy."

William leaped out of the window and after the voice that called to him. His bare feet landed on the crunchy grass, and although it chilled him on the inside, it felt quite good.

Once he landed outside, William was met with confusion. Although he was a strong, tall, and sturdy thirteen-year-old boy, bigger than the majority of his friends, and had been taught well to stand up for himself, he knew he shouldn't have been out there. Yet, the voice pulled him closer, a magnetic field bracing for his landing.

"How can I help you?" William called out.

"Commee here, William. Just a little bit closer now, boy."

William knew right then where the voice was coming from. The voice called to him from the berry bush just past his family's backyard. The berry bush looked odd, though. The berries seemed to have gone purple and black and rotted away. He took a large step over to the bush when a blue, disgusting hand shocked him, grabbing his frilly shirt collar.

The hand pulled him in with incredible strength so he had no choice but to give in. Then the other hand shot out and ripped him into the tattered, now black berry bush.

In a brief instant, William found himself staring at something his eyes couldn't quite believe. Its skin was shiny and blue, and it wore a large black bowler hat. If he wasn't mistaken, William would say this was a witch.

"Good evening, William," Bramilda the blue witch said. "The Watcher will see you now, he he he he he." She dragged poor William off into the night, never to be seen again.

That wasn't exactly true, though. It wasn't until about 130 years later, when William had eroded into a small stone trapped forever in the Watcher's evil underground cave of horrors, was he seen again. Although he was now trapped inside the patchy satchel of the evil monster, he was seen. He was found. And it was by the most peculiar trio of children. For that, William was grateful.

41

Gramilda and Bramilda, the evil twin witches, were hard at work in their own tiny section of the underground cave of horrors. Their room of the house of horrors was mostly dark, the only light coming from a black cauldron in the middle of the room with glowing, green content bubbling and popping up.

The walls were lined top to bottom with ingredients stored in various mason jars and vials of all sizes. Gramilda grabbed a small vial of black liquid off the wall, ripped off its wooden topper, and poured the contents into the cauldron. A heap of black smoke whooshed out of the cauldron. "He he he he he." Gramilda let out the evilest laugh.

"It's been so long, sister. We haven't done this one in what feels like forever," Bramilda said.

"It's almost ready, evil sister, he he he he." Gramilda scoured the walls of ingredients, looking to put the final touches on their potion, when she spotted the juicy treat crawling up the wall. It was so large and so delicious.

"Mmmmm, a bulbous bug." Gramilda scowled. "My favorite."

The bug was out of her reach, so she stood up tall on her tippy toes, reaching out with her long fingers, but it was still just out of reach and crawling farther away. Gramilda stepped up onto the first wooden shelf of her ingredient wall and reached even farther up to grab it, but it was crawling away. Slowly, but it was inching out of her reach. Gramilda climbed one shelf higher and reached as far as she could, one final stretch while licking her lips, but instead of getting her grabby hands on her dinner, she clumsily fell backward, and with her came the entire wall of ingredients.

Glass shattered, vials clinked to the floor, juices and ingredients were strewn everywhere. Gramilda poked her head up from the rubble and laid her eyes on the bug that had tumbled down to the floor with the rest of the shelf. Her eyes watered, and her mouth salivated. Gramilda took one motion up and out of the crash when she saw her sister bend down to the ground and slurp up the massive bulbous bug with no hands.

"Nice try, sister, he he he he he!" Bramilda said, letting out a gargled burp. "Most delicious," she said, licking her fingers.

Gramilda's eyes were fiery as she finally made it up and out from the floor of broken wall. She took one step over to her sister, Bramilda, ready to make her anger known, when she saw the final ingredient in her peripheral vision. The mason jar contained a bright yellow gas that swirled in cyclonic motion within. A smile formed on her mouth, as Gramilda the witch grabbed the jar off the ground, twisted open its top, and took a long whiff for good measure.

Gramilda threw the entire jar into the cauldron and watched as the contents within morphed from a dark green to a shrieking, fluorescent yellow. Both sisters looked at each other and knew they had completed their potion.

Walking up to the base of the cauldron, the evil twin witch sisters stood opposite each other. They took a long look at each other before dropping their entire faces into the cauldron's yellow liquid. They slurped up giant mouthfuls of the potion, pulled their heads back and out, yellow liquid seeping down their lips.

Gramilda and Bramilda instantly knew the potency of their potion. They radiated delight and took another long glance at each other before letting out an evil, snarling laugh in unison.

42

Emmy, Jack, and Sam entered the cave, and the feelings of dread came rushing back into them. The jelly monster, the witches, the monsters, the evil creations, the children, the Watcher, and all the in-between whisked through their minds at warp speed.

"Here, take this," Sam said, handing the bag of supplies over to Jack.

"I wish we didn't have to do this," Jack took off his ghost costume and pulled the backpack over his shoulders.

"But we do have to do this," Emmy said.

Sam stood silently. He kept his demeanor fierce; his tone said everything his friends needed to know. Although Emmy and Jack were haunted by the horrors in the underground cave, Sam had felt the death grip of the evil being. Only he really knew of the true horrors that existed in the cave. He tightened his grip on the baseball bat.

"Okay, so which cavern do we try this time?" Jack

called out.

"Eeny, meeny, meiny, mo?" Emmy replied.

"That one," Sam said sternly, pointing over to a cave that looked just like the rest.

"Why that one?" Jack asked.

"It's just a feeling," Sam said.

"All right, we follow Sam's lead," Emmy said. "Oh, wait!"

"What is it, Emmy?"

"Shoelaces. They're in the bag, please," Emmy pointed.

"Good call," Jack said, unstrapping the book bag to the floor and pulling out the garbled bundle of shoelaces Emmy had brought.

Emmy grabbed the laces and trekked back to the mouth of the cave and began laying down her breadcrumbs.

"Hey, you okay?" Jack sat down next to Sam, picking up on his eerie quietness.

"I'm okay," Sam said hesitatingly.

A brief moment of silence before Sam spoke again. "It's just being back down here," he said. "I still feel him. There's a part of his evil that will always be with me. And being down here just sets it off. It's like my body starts to run cold, and the feeling of doom washes over me again."

"We're going to end this, together," Jack said, putting his hand on Sam's shoulder. "And, hey, we might even have time for a scary movie later."

Jack was the best of friends, Sam knew. The two had met pretty much the day they were born, and Sam wouldn't take on this adventure without his best friend by his side.

"Fine, but only if it's mega scary, and we can force Emmy to watch it," Sam said, a half smile forming on his lips.

"Yeah. Duh!" Jack replied. "Hey, maybe we can glue her in her sleeping bag!"

"And tape her eyes open!" Sam said.

Sam and Jack laughed heartily, and that felt great. The thought of normalcy—well, normalcy for them—triggered all the emotions. The two bumped fists in approval.

"Okay, all set with the laces. What are you two rambling on about?" Emmy said.

"Oh, uh. Nothing. Just guy talk. Are you ready?" Jack said.

"Yeah, uh-huh. Sounds like it. Whatever, dingus. We're all good on laces. Over and out," Emmy said.

"Copy that," Sam said, and the three walked on into the darkness of the cave.

43

The Watcher stood up from his throne of clocks and walked over to a long, tall, wooden treelike structure that held a perfectly round clock on its top. The stand came up to the Watcher's waist and was made up of twisted barks of dark browns and purples. The Watcher waved one long finger around the clock at the top, circling it with a green glow of energy, his evil power at work.

After several swirls, the clock rippled into a mirrorlike image of the three children. Acting as a powerful crystal ball, the clock showed the children's whereabouts. The Watcher looked on as the children lined the cave's entrance with shoelaces.

"Ha ha ha ha ha. Pathetic," the Watcher said to himself. "It's such a shame they are volunteering their own doom. To brave my cave and come down to challenge me, the greatest evil that ever lived, with nothing more than shoelaces?" The thought brought the Watcher sheer bliss.

His moment of joy was interrupted by two voices, two human voices briskly festering down into his chamber. He was, however, about to be even more pleased.

"Sister, you look breathtaking as a child!" the voice of Emmy called out to Jack.

"A boy! I've always wanted to be a boy, he he he he," the voice of Jack said to Emmy.

Looking on as the fake Emmy and Jack approached, the Watcher knew immediately the delightful plan that was being put in place. "You look magnificent!" the Watcher said, as the evil twin witch sisters walked closer, the effects of their potion clear.

"Why, thank you master," Gramilda, disguised as Emmy, said.

"Yes, these kids are doomed he he he he," Bramilda, disguised as Jack, said.

"Your heinous ways never cease to amaze me, my minions." The Watcher bowed toward the witches, again showing his approval for their work. "Now, go. Put an end to their insufferable attempt to stop us. And bring them to me. I want them . . . to suffer."

"Yes, master!" the witches chimed in unison before turning around to head off the children.

"Oh, wait. One more thing," the Watcher said, grabbing at the thin, patchy satchel at his side. "Take this dreadful thing. Get it out of my sight. Let him watch and hear the suffering from up close." The Watcher handed the satchel holding Stony to Gramilda, disguised as Emmy.

Stony squirmed inside and lopped around, trying to break free, but his efforts were for naught.

Grabbing the satchel, Gramilda and Bramilda ran off to thwart the rescue plan of Sam, Emmy, and Jack. Their human legs pumped up and down, an incredible feeling they thought they could get used to.

44

Sam, Emmy, and Jack marched on together through the dark cave. They were very much unsure of the horrors yet to be encountered down in the cavern, but they had one another, and that was more than most.

"I wish Stony were here," Emmy said.

"Me, too," Jack responded. "But we are going to find him."

The cave they were walking in was impossibly dark. The faint light from the cavern opening, back where they had entered, was a distant memory.

Sam opened up his cell phone to shine the light around and see something, anything, but all around him was black. The hard floors, the walls, they were all the darkest of blacks. He moved the light over to Emmy and Jack, who were behind him, trudging along slowly.

Emmy grabbed some shoelace out of her pocket and laid it down along the dark cavern wall.

Jack had his hands in his pockets. "Hey, that's too bright!" he said, his eyes unable to adjust to the bright white of Sam's phone's light.

"Sorry, it's just so dark in this cave. I thought my eyes would adjust, but I can't see anything," Sam replied.

"Hey, watch it, dingus!" Emmy called out.

"Watch what?" Jack replied.

"You know what," Emmy said.

"No, I really don't."

Sam shined his phone light back at Emmy, who was trailing behind Jack about ten feet.

"Whatever, dingus," Emmy said, walking on through the darkness.

Sam moved his phone light back around facing out forward, leading the pack onward through the cave.

It wasn't more than a minute later when Emmy called out again, "I swear, dingus! If you grab my shoulders one more time!"

Sam, again, whipped his light around and shined it on Emmy, who was even farther behind him and Jack now.

"I seriously don't know what you're talking about," Jack said.

Emmy realized how far she had fallen behind her friends when Sam shined the light back on her. There was no way Jack could have been close enough to grab her.

Gulping in fear, Emmy spoke. "Uh, guys? I'm not so sure we're alone down here."

"GAHHHHHH!" Jack yelled out as something

grabbed his shoulders, lifting him several inches into the air.

Sam whipped his phone to where Jack was standing. Jack immediately dropped to the floor and landed on his feet. "Are you okay?" Sam said.

"Something grabbed me!" Jack trembled.

"AAAAAAHHHHHHH!!" Emmy's bloodcurdling scream, and the scraping of dirt along the cave floor, alarmed Jack and Sam.

Sam whipped his phone's light back at Emmy, who was on the floor, belly down, a droplet gathering at the corner of her eye.

Emmy rapidly stood back up. "We have to get out of here."

Then the same high-pitched scream came from Sam's peripheral, as Jack, too, was dragged along the dirt-lined cave floor. When Sam shined the light over to where Jack was, he, too, was belly down on the dirt.

"Something was pulling my ankle!" Jack yelled out.

"It's the light!" Emmy said. "They can't be in the light!"

Emmy was right about whatever "they" were.

Emmy and Jack ripped out their phones from their pockets and followed in Sam's lead. The three ran to one another, stood back-to-back, and shined their lights all around the cave. There was nothing.

"Okay, slowly and one step at a time," Sam said.

"Keep the light still," Emmy replied. "If we keep our backs to each other, and keep the light shined outward, we might have a chance."

Then the whispers started. All around them, the three best friends heard frightening whispers.

"Grab them!" one voice hissed.

"I can't, it's too bright!" another replied.

"Grab the girl! The ankles!"

"Squash them!"

"Crumple them to dust!"

"Snatch them now!"

"Let's eat them!"

The voices all hissed and spoke over one another, like tiny mice fighting over their dinner.

Emmy thought she saw a shadow reach out from the darkness and pull back from the light, but she also had trouble comprehending if it was reality or not.

Eventually, the whispers grew to full-blown chatter. All around them, they could hear the creatures snarling and wishing them dead in all types of ways. Mostly unbearable and horrible.

And then, they saw them. Their eyes began adjusting to the dim of the light shining all around them, as they walked step by step. There the creatures were in the darkness just on the outskirts of the light. The creatures were nothing more than shadows, black ghosts with empty eye holes cascading over one another, trying to reach Emmy, Sam, and Jack.

Luckily, the friends realized just in the nick of time that it was the light they couldn't touch.

Keeping their wits close and one another closer, they continued on through the darkness of the cave until they reached a brighter domain. The whispers died down and the three besties regained their composure, moving their positions away from one another.

"Welp, cross evil shadow monsters who are scared of the light off our list," Emmy said while she laid down breadcrumb shoelaces. "This will be fun on our way back."

The trio looked at one another and kept moving on in their quest.

45

The Watcher bid his witches off and sauntered back over to his crystal-ball clock. With a wave of his finger, the face of the clock again whirred, and the image of Sam, Jack, and Emmy appeared.

He looked on and listened as the shadow monsters' whispers flooded his senses, one of them grabbing the girl's ankle and pulling her into the shadows. A smirk formed on his face. "Yes, most excellent. How dare you come down to my domain and think you can defeat me?" the Watcher called out to his crystal ball. "You don't stand a chance, foolish children!"

But then, a quick and decisive act from one of the young boys shining the light at the shadow monsters and saving his friend made the Watcher scowl. The Watcher then looked on in disgust as the three best friends merged together with their backs facing outward, shining lights in all directions, and eventually heading out of the cavern of shadow monsters.

The Watcher slammed a massive fist down onto his

crystal-ball clock, nearly shattering it. "Malfeasance!" he exclaimed, furious at the contents within the crystal-ball clock.

The Watcher calmed himself, took a deep breath in, and instantly regained his composure. "No matter. It's a pity you will fail, stupid little children!"

Stepping back and away from his crystal ball, the Watcher again displayed his evil prowess. The Watcher raised an arm slowly but with a purpose, his entire arm a green glow of electricity. Slowly, the Watcher lifted his arm into the air and chanted, "Grow, minions. Rise up from the ground and do my bidding. Go now and destroy those kids!"

And with his chant, the Watcher roared into a fit of laughter that rattled the walls of his domain.

46

"Let's see what's behind door number three, Bob!" Emmy said, taking in her new surroundings. The besties found themselves in a new and brighter path.

"Maybe we're safe in this cave," Jack hoped.

"We're too close," Sam said. "He knows we're here. We can't be sure of anything."

Jack bent down to examine the new cavern. The ground beneath them slowly moved from smooth and grainy to an uneven and rocky terrain. It was littered with rocks of all different sizes. "It's all rocky."

"At least there's no jelly," Emmy said.

"You got that right," Jack added.

"These rocks remind me of Stony," Emmy picked a rather large rock up off the ground.

"He's here, Emmy. Somewhere." Jack put his hand on her shoulder for comfort. "We're going to find him."

Emmy knew Jack was right. She knew that they had braved so much together in such a small amount of time. They had to find him, they just had to. There was no other option. *Right?* But then, a dark and horrible thought crossed her mind. *What if I am wrong?* What if they failed, and the Watcher turned them into dribbling, soulless children to work his clock tower forever? What if she never saw her mom again? What if her memories of Jack and Sam were stolen from her? She shoved those thoughts away, knowing her friends needed her and focused her attention back to the task at hand.

"I know we will," Emmy said.

After a few more steps, a parting of gravel cracked and opened in between a section of the ground with massive rocks. A fog of green light shined up from the opening in front of the kids.

"I think I may have been wrong," Jack said, panicking.

"What else is new, dingus?" Emmy responded, her senses refreshed and an icy demeanor on her face as she stared at the green light.

"Get ready!" Sam said, watching as skeleton hands crept over the lip of the hole in the ground.

Up from the green tint and the soil, skeletons emerged. The Watcher's minions trundled up and out of the opening, racing toward Emmy, Sam, and Jack, waddling their legs back and forth.

Sam fearlessly raced up to the first skeleton and rocked it back with a forceful swing of his baseball bat, knocking off one of its arms in the process.

"Way to go, Sam!" Emmy said.

"That was awesome!" Jack responded and followed suit. He then ran up to one of the skeletons and whomped it with the back of his arms, launching it into the wall.

"Hey, you guys are crushing it! Keep it going." Emmy said.

"Your turn, Emmy!" Sam launched an attack at another skeleton making its way over to him.

Emmy turned around and saw one of the creatures plodding along, step by skeletal step getting closer. She reared her legs, which had been primed from a ton of running down in the cave, back. When the skeleton got close enough, she primed herself and launched a kick that sent the skeleton flying backward and down onto the rocky ground.

The kids continued their attack on the Watcher's minions until about two dozen were lying on the floor, motionless.

"CAKE!" Jack said. "I think I'm starting to get the hang of beating these monsters."

"That was AWESOME!" Emmy said. "Did you guys see that kick? I annihilated it!"

Sam wanted to join in on the fun, but a dark, ominous feeling came over him, as it had many times before. Something told him this was too easy.

"Hey, skeletons," Jack said. "We've got a bone to pick with you!"

Emmy let out a good belly laugh.

Sam looked around, ignoring the laughter coming from his friends. *What's the catch?* he thought to himself. He knew there was something else, something eviler about these skeletons. And then, their evilness showed itself, as one skeleton's body gravitated back up from the ground and again stood on its two wobbly legs.

"Hey, guys?" Sam said.

"Yo, skeletons, why you acting so hollow lately?" Jack continued piling on the jokes.

And Emmy continued on with the belly laughs.

"GUYS!" Sam shouted even louder this time to get the attention of his two best friends.

Jack and Emmy heard Sam, looked over, and the laughing stopped immediately.

The skeletons were rising back up; limb by limb, they were levitating back on their two feet. It wouldn't be long before the entire army was back up and in hot pursuit of Sam, Emmy and Jack. They could try to fend them off again, but then what? Would they keep rising over and over? This didn't seem like it would end well for the three friends.

"Jack, quick! Let's do it!" Emmy called out, running over to a skeleton and bumping it back into the wall and down to the ground. Emmy cut her arm in the process. The skeleton seemed a little harder to move this time, slightly stronger after being brought back.

Jack followed her lead and instantly realized the same thing. He was still able to wallop them down to the ground with force, but it wasn't as easy this time. They had become stronger from regenerating.

Sam helped, too; his bat a tool of destruction, smacking the creatures down to the ground.

On the trio went pushing, shoving, and hitting the skeletons all around them until once again they were free and clear of the baddies.

"There, that ought to do it," Jack said, panting and out of breath.

The regeneration happened even quicker this time. Within seconds, the skeletons started rising again, up on their feet and slowly marching toward them. But this time, Jack noticed that there seemed to be meat hanging off their frames. They weren't just bones anymore. Jack noticed the skeletons had grown muscle, and it formed on their bones like moss on a tree.

Going through the process again and even more winded this time, Sam, Emmy, and Jack defeated the skeletons. "We need to find a different way!" Sam said.

"Let's run for it!" Emmy noticed the skeletons already rising back up, their bony frames gaining more and more substance. Now, the skeletons had mass. Red strands of muscle and tissue made up the now not-so-hollow insides lining their bones. It also made them much harder to knock down.

"We can't!" Jack said. "They are all around us now, blocking the exit."

Running had been somewhat of a fallback plan for Emmy and Jack up to that point. They had relied on their legs many times before in the cave, but this time, they would have to use their wits if they were going to survive.

Jack ran up to a skeleton and shoved it so hard, he

fell backward to the ground. The skeleton didn't budge. They were too powerful now, filled with too much muscle.

"What do we do?!" Sam said.

"I don't know, but we better do it fast," Emmy replied.

Sam ran up to a skeleton and hit a direct shot with his bat, but the thing, again, didn't budge.

The skeletons inched in closer, all around them now. Their massive chest cavities, filled with muscle, heaved in and out with each step.

"I wish Stony were here!" Emmy called out.

"Quick, the stones!" Sam said, Emmy's words sparking his idea. "Throw the rocks!"

All around them, the three besties started launching rocks at the skeletons. Rocks of all sizes and shapes. Most simply hit the muscle mass or bone and bounced off. "I don't think it's working," Jack said.

Sam gathered himself. The skeletons were now merely a few feet away and completely surrounded them. Sam bent his knees, reared back, and prepared for a mondo swing to the Moon from his bat. He swung heavily, with all his might, at an approaching skeleton, and it was a direct hit. The swing of the bat had completely knocked the skeleton's head clean off its body. The skeleton dropped to the floor and vanished into a gust of gray wind.

"It's the head!" Sam yelled. "You have to knock off its head!"

A sense of relief washed over the group.

Emmy and Jack worked together, picking a large rock off the ground and nailing a nearby skeleton directly above the shoulders. It, too, crashed down to the ground in a sea of bones and oozy, red muscle mass, then dispersed into a gray gust of gas.

Realizing they didn't necessarily need the rocks or the bat, as their heads popped off quite easily, Sam, Emmy, and Jack began knocking heads off all around them. The cavern filled with clouds of gray smoke as they defeated each skeleton one by one.

In just a short period of time, the skeletons were no more, and the trio of heroes moved onward.

47

"SNIVELING DRITS!!" the Watcher shrieked, pounding another fist down onto his crystal-ball clock. "Clever little ones."

The Watcher lifted his gaze and walked back over to his throne of clocks to ponder. He sat down, then stood back up. He sat down again, then stood back up.

"These filthy kids are beginning to get on my nerves!"

The Watcher walked away from his throne and over to the source of his power at the end of his inner domain. He looked on at the massive clock tower, at his all-too-powerful display. He watched the pale, soulless children grind and switch, press and jam everywhere. A smile formed on his snout.

Feeling his powers course through his body, the Watcher reminded himself again that he was on the verge of succeeding. The world above would soon belong to him once again. He reminded himself of Gramilda and Bramilda, who were on their way over to those disgusting children right now. He reminded himself that he was the one who had brought the children here. He reminded himself that he was the one with the power to collect the souls of children, he was the one to summon monsters and, if need be, he would be the one to put an end to their silly little adventure.

The Watcher's smirk grew even wider now, and he let out a deep laugh from the pits of his scaly stomach. It echoed through the entire cavern, as clocks all around him tinked and fell to the ground.

48

"Did you hear that?" Sam looked at his friends as the Watcher's laugh rattled the cavern they were in. The trio had marched on well past the skeletons now. Their new surroundings didn't have much in the way of a clue or direction. It was simply a dirt-filled cave.

"We must be close," Emmy said.

"I don't think I want to be close." Jack gulped.

"Of course, you want to be close, dingus," Emmy replied.

"No, I just don't want to be close to you," Jack said. "Your breath smells like a fart."

Emmy couldn't help but laugh. "Oh, I thought that was your favorite scent?" Emmy said, running over to Jack and pushing a hot brush of her breath into Jack's face.

Jack had no time to react, and he tripped over his back foot and down to the dirt floor beneath him, taking Emmy with him.

The two again found themselves staring into each

other's eyes, lying on the cavern floor.

In that moment, the rest of the world seemed like a disappearing act. Sam, Stony, the Watcher, the witches, the clock tower: none of it mattered. Lying on the floor of that disgusting, dirty cave, Emmy felt only the most wonderful thing. Jack felt it, too.

"Your breath actually smells kind of nice," Jack said.

"Oh, well thank you, dingus. I'm glad it doesn't smell like a fart," Emmy said, as she found her face gravitating closer toward Jack's.

"No, it kind of smells like . . ."

"JELLY!" the two friends yelled in unison, immediately launching back up to their feet.

"Is that a bad thing?" Sam said.

"Yes, it's a very bad thing," Jack said. "We need to go, quickly."

Emmy laid down some shoelace, and the three friends picked up their pace, running down the cave. The smell of the jelly only became more prominent.

"It's getting worse!" Emmy said. "It's wafting into my nostrils, and it smells so good."

"Emmy, keep focused! It's him, it's the jelly monster. He has to be around here somewhere."

Having no choice but to move forward, the friends kept on running until they were stopped by the same *squish* and *gunk* under their feet that Emmy and Jack were all too familiar with.

"Sam!" Emmy yelled, pumping her legs up and down in rapid succession. "You have to keep moving your feet."

"The ground will suck you down," Jack replied. "Do not stay in one spot, keep your legs moving!"

"COPY!" Sam said, joining in and lifting one leg after the other. "High knees, high knees!" he called out.

And in an instant, the mountain of goo erupted from the cave floor, and again Emmy and Jack, now joined by their bestie, Sam, found themselves staring face-to-face with the cascading pile of jelly.

"Keep moving and watch out for the black goo!" Jack called out to his friends.

The jelly monster let out a long screech, the smells of peach, blueberry, and orange shooting through the kids like the scent of pie fresh out of the oven.

The jelly monster reared back and launched a steaming pile of black goo at Sam, who jumped out of the way and rolled on the cavern floor. He picked himself back up and kept hoisting his feet up and down. The spot where the black goo had landed hissed and burned, creating a sizeable hole in the dirt floor.

Jack ripped the bag of supplies off his shoulders, kept his feet pumping, and took out the slingshot he had packed. He knew there wasn't much hope, but maybe if he could launch something into its eye, he might have a chance. Jack took in his surroundings. Although the cave was mostly smooth and clear, there were still rocks littered throughout the dirt and gravel. Scouring around him, Jack picked up several and started loading his wrist rocket.

"Aim for the eyes!" Sam said, panting while trying to keep his legs pumping up and down.

Jack launched several rocks. The first few landed on the head and body of the jelly monster with a *glub* sound and quickly sank into the viscous liquid that made up the monster.

Then Jack took the most careful aim and launched one of his last rocks directly into the eye of the jelly monster. Unfortunately for him, the jelly monster's eye was unfazed. Just like it happened with the rest of its body, the rock *glubbed* right into it and disappeared.

"What do we do now?!" Sam said.

"Let's run for it!" Emmy replied.

The jelly monster was blocking their way forward through the cave, so they needed to backtrack. They didn't know what monsters could await them there, but it had to be better than this.

The trio pumped their legs and ran back the way they came, but the jelly monster sunk into the ground and reemerged on the other side to stop them. Immediately when it rose up, putting an end to their retreat backward, it launched another heaping pile of goo at Emmy. She screamed and ducked as it whizzed above her and hissed against the cave wall.

The jelly monster now closed in on Jack, who had nowhere to turn to. The monster had gotten smarter. Jack's back was toward the cave wall, and his entire surroundings were capped off and blocked by the jelly monster.

Emmy and Sam looked on in fear, still moving their legs up and down. There was nothing they could do; the jelly monster was about to end Jack.

Inching closer, the jelly monster reared back and prepared to launch black goo at Jack, which would surely be his end.

Jack, looking in both directions and understanding there was no escape, took his backpack off and launched it at the jelly monster in a final act of desperation. It *glubbed* and was consumed by it, just like the rocks he had tried.

Jack scowled in fear, closing one eye in hopes that whatever the jelly monster was about to do to him, it would happen quickly. He thought of Sam, he thought of his parents, he thought of the Watcher, but most importantly, he thought of Emmy. As he sat there, shrunken in fear and about to meet his demise by the hands of the evil jelly monster, Jack thought about the moment he had shared with Emmy just a few minutes ago. Lying on the cave floor, face-to-face, Jack realized he had a huge crush on his best friend, Emmy.

And just then, before it even had a chance to spew out its goo, the jelly monster belched and gurgled. It was a deep sound that came from far down in the depths of its body. The smell that came out wasn't of delicious jellies but of rot and ruin. The jelly monster backed away from Jack, again belching grossly. The jelly monster's body, which was made of a rainbow of colors flowing endlessly, was rapidly turning to rich browns.

Jack noticed it also seemed to be shrinking. In just moments, what was previously a large, hulking rainbow of force had shrunk down to a brown pile of thick substance, not any bigger than a dog. It kept shrinking and gurgling until it simply evaporated.

The jellies and smells all around them evaporated along with it.

The three friends gathered in close to one another in a semicircle, shoulder to shoulder. They looked down at the small stain of brown that had been left on the cave floor from the jelly monster.

"What did you do?" Emmy said.

"I don't know, I just threw my bag at it," Jack responded, holding the slingshot in his hand.

"What was in your bag?" Sam said.

"Just some stuff. Phone charger, batteries, hoodie . . ." And then it hit Jack like a sack of bricks. "A peanut butter sandwich."

49

Up above on the surface of Mill Falls, chaos was ensuing. Skeletons ran roughshod in the quaint neighborhoods, gathering children, turning them into tiny skeletal statues to bring back down into the underground cave, to bring back down to their master, the Watcher.

The Watcher's evilest minions—the pumpkin, mummy, and troll—continued wreaking havoc as well. They hopped along in unison, house to house, bouncing to each neighborhood, trick-or-treating for their own candy. Trick-or-treating for children. The troll held a large sack of booger children by his side. The mummy stuffed his victims into his own wrappings. The pumpkin, bobbing along on his incredibly eerie, stalk-like legs, stored his earnings in a satchel by his side.

A small gathering of parents looked on at the ghastly sight, their children previously captured by the three evil monsters.

"N-n-now, w-w-we d-d-don't want any trouble, okay?" George Álvarez said to the troll, mummy, and pumpkin, as a small group of parents sheepishly formed behind him, cowering in fright.

George was staring directly at the pumpkin's satchel by his side. Just moments ago, the pumpkin had done *something* to his boy, Alfie. George couldn't quite explain what the pumpkin had done because, gosh darn, it just didn't make any sense. One minute his boy was there, and the next he was not. He remembered the orange and green lights, and the pumpkin picking a rather large pumpkin seed right up off the floor where his boy had just been standing. But again, that didn't make any sense.

"Yeah, give us back our kids!" another parent shouted at the monsters, raising one arm for emphasis. The parent seemed to be all talk, though, as she carefully backpedaled to the far back of the group.

"N-n-now, l-l-like I said," George Álvarez stammered. "We already called the police, you hear?"

George looked at the three monstrosities. *These things can hear, right?* He didn't even see ears on the mummy or pumpkin. He thought he saw small ears pocketed under gobs of snot on the troll's head. "We don't want any trouble, but we're going to need our children back. So with the police on their way, I don't think that gives you much of a choice, you hear?"

The monstrosities looked at one another and giggled. The troll tapped his side sack for good measure, taunting George and his crew.

"S-s-so, i-i-it's like this," George went on. "You have two options, as I see it. You either give us our children back now, and we'll go on our way. Or those coppers will arrive any minute and make this a whole lot more difficult for you."

The troll looked at the other two monsters, again let out a giggle, and pulled out his small ax. The parents gasped and took several steps back.

In a flash, the troll sent out a large, heaping spray of snot from his weapon. It covered the small group of parents entirely, wrestling them to the ground. It formed an adhesive blanket covering their bodies, gluing them to the ground.

"Hey, you idiot! Let us out of here!" George Álvarez wiggled side to side in the snotty cocoon, and his glasses were all lopsided on his face. The rest of the parents rambled incoherent nonsense to his left and right, also doing their best to wiggle free, to no avail.

The troll took several steps up to the smattering of parents stuck to the asphalt road. He bent down and, with one finger, scooped up a gob of snot from off the gooey blanket holding them down, a child sneaking a taste of birthday cake.

He stuck his finger in his mouth, slurping up the disgusting, green substance. His face donned a large smile as he and the other monsters eagerly walked on to a different house and a different neighborhood, giggling like tiny children on Halloween night.

About a mile down the road, a Mill Falls police cruiser was stuck on the side of the road. The vehicle was mostly beat up, shattered windows and popped tires. The red-and-blue flashing lights were still on, where just a few minutes prior, the two police officers had run screaming as a skeleton had made its way over to them and chased them away.

50

"Go, figure," Emmy said. "Peanut butter! That's all it took. For once, your hunger may have saved us, dingus."

"A jelly monster that's allergic to peanut butter. This is something else." Sam snickered at the hilarity of it all.

Emmy reached down deep into her pockets and pulled out some more shoelace. "Running low. I hope we're close."

"We are close," Sam said.

Emmy and Jack looked at each other.

"How do you know?" Jack said.

"I just do, I can feel it." Sam looked down at his feet. "Like I said, it's just this feeling, deep down inside me. It's like a hunch, and it grows whenever he's near. Like right now."

"Who needs shoelaces when we have you, Sam?" Emmy said.

"It's not making it to him that we need to worry about it. He's expecting us. It's finding our way out of here that we need to worry about. If . . . if we make it that far." Sam looked at his two best friends, lips churned down in a half smile.

"Well, we didn't come this far to worry about that now," Jack called out. "We just beat the darn jelly monster! This is a time for celebration!" Jack grabbed Emmy by her hands and whisked her around in celebration.

"Yeah, celebration," Sam whispered to no one but himself. He knew the jelly monster was the smallest of victories, as they were getting closer. The feeling loomed over him with great force now.

And on they went.

The celebration died down, and Sam, Jack, and Emmy went through the motions of another few caverns. Walking and laying down shoelace, walking and laying down shoelace. Emmy began putting down less and less shoelace in an effort to conserve.

"My legs hurt," Emmy said. "Too much running. Too much walking."

"Well, how does your face feel?" Jack said.

"My face? My face feels fine, why do you ask?" Emmy replied.

"Because it's killing me!" Jack barely laughed at his own joke, knowing it was a dud.

"Ha. Good one, dingus. Did you make that one up all by yourself?"

It was just then, in that very moment, when Sam heard the clock. The faint but distinct tick of a nearby clock. The three best friends were no longer close. They were very close. The Watcher was upon them. Sam could feel it.

51

"I'm not sure I'll ever change back!" Bramilda said, still gushing over her new bearings, running side sprints back and forth. The body of Jack pleased her very much. She was quick, fast, and limber.

"Pipe down, sister," Gramilda said, but it wasn't her voice speaking, of course. It was the voice of her new form, Emmy. "The potion doesn't last forever. We only have a short time before the effects wear off, so we must act now."

"Ugh, can't it wait?" Bramilda said. "I'm hungry!"

"You're always hungry, Brimmy," Gramilda replied.

"Shhh," Bramilda cut her sister off. "Sister . . ."

A smile formed on the mouth of Gramilda, the green-skinned witch, although now the face of a young middle-school girl. "Marveeelous," she said, as the chatter of the real Sam, Emmy, and Jack could be heard just down the cavern.

52

Emmy, Sam, and Jack all heard it, actually. They all heard the soft tick of a clock somewhere not far in the distance. A cold shudder ran through each of them. This was their goal, indeed, to find the Watcher, take down his clock tower, and put an end to his reign of terror. And now they were closer than ever. However, they just didn't know how they would accomplish their goal, and they were surely terrified they would end up like those other children, the very ones they were trying to save.

"We need to keep moving, I can feel him. We are close. This way." Sam motioned them over in the direction he'd heard the clock.

Jack was practicing with his slingshot, pulling the rubber band back and launching air repeatedly. He nodded and followed along.

Emmy followed suit as well, trying to fix one of her fairy wings that had just about run its course. Maybe it happened back at their showdown with the jelly monster, but one of her wings had completely bent in half. She had had enough and tried to take the pair of wings off. They were attached by a simple clasp on the back part of her suit. She tried several times before giving up.

"Hey, you need some help?" Jack said, taking a break from his slingshot.

"That would be swell," Emmy replied.

The two stopped walking, and Jack made his way closer to Emmy. "Turn around," he said.

Emmy followed Jack's directions and waited patiently while he helped with her costume. Jack carefully placed one hand on the clasp, doing his best to work it open. His other hand, however had found its way onto Emmy's neck. Jack felt the smoothness of Emmy's neck, wisps of hair falling down over his hand, as he worked the clasp free. Before he even had a chance to lift the clasp up and take the wings off, Emmy turned around.

"Jack?" Emmy said.

In a sudden and swift motion—although Jack had no idea what he was thinking or what he was doing—he laid a big kiss on Emmy's lips. He let his lips stay there, lost in the moment. He had been thinking about this very thing for a long time. But something was wrong. He tried to remove his face from Emmy's, but he was stuck. His lips felt like they were glued to hers. Jack pulled back even harder, his lips stretching out from Emmy's face, and finally he was able to remove them and look at Emmy.

"Mmmm, delicious little boy," Emmy spat back.

"Emmy?" Jack said.

"What's up, dingus?" Emmy called out, but the voice didn't come from the person standing in front of him. It came from behind him. Jack quickly turned around and saw Emmy. *But that's impossible.* "What's up?" Emmy said, running back over to Jack while still grasping and reaching at the clasp on her back.

"Come back, boy! You taste so delicious, and I'm so hungry, he he he he!" Gramilda, disguised as Emmy, said.

The real Emmy looked over at the fake Emmy in horror. "Hey, Sam?" Emmy said to her friend. "I think we've got company."

Sam jumped out of the shadows, ducked, and rolled along the floor as a long cackle of green lightning just missed him by a hair. "It's the witches!" Sam yelled.

Bramilda the witch, disguised as Jack, popped out from behind the shadows she was hiding in. "Greetings, besties!" she said. "Halloween-sleepover weekend! Tubular, he he he he."

Bramilda lifted up her finger, the finger of Jack, and pointed it at the ceiling, a snap of green electricity ripping out and hitting a small protrusion. It fell to the ground, but Sam evaded it and rolled over to his friends.

Standing back-to-back, the friends looked out at the two witch things that had greeted them. The Jack clone was behind them, and the Emmy clone was in front of them. They had nowhere to go.

"Come back, Jack! I am *so* hungry, and you tasted so

delicious, he he he."

The two witches leaped in and met their twins in a grapple, grabbing Emmy and Jack by the shoulders, wrestling them around in a loop the loop. Their action had forced Sam away from their back-to-back position.

Sam backed up and watched in terror as the witches, Jack, and Emmy all twisted around, do-si-doing, a whirlwind of confusion. *Who is who?*

The circling had stopped, and both versions of Jack and Emmy looked back at Sam. The two Jacks and the two Emmys looked identical.

Sam looked them up and down; there was nothing, not a single, minuscule difference. He gasped in horror. *Who are my real friends?* He hadn't felt a horribly lonely moment like this since he was trapped as one of the Watcher's minions. Sam lifted his trusty bat, rearing it as if to launch a swing at the witches. *But who are the witches?*

"Help, Sam!" one of the Emmys called out.

"No, help *me*, Sam!" the other Emmy shouted, trying to better the first Emmy.

"Don't believe her, Sam!" one of the Jacks said.

"Believe me, Sam!" the other Jack said. "It's him! He's the witch!"

Sam couldn't believe what he was seeing; this was a nightmare. He had to figure out who his real friends were.

The other friends grappled with one another again, wrestling around Jack to Jack and Emmy to Emmy. Spinning in tight circles, there was simply no way for

Sam to know who was who.

The spinning stopped, and Sam looked down at the ground. He was distraught. He was so confused, and he couldn't look to his friends for help because he didn't know who his real friends were. Sam needed to think of something, anything. Maybe he could ask them a question that only the real Jack and Emmy would know? No, surely the witches would have accounted for this and would know the answers. That wouldn't work.

"Help us, Sam. Please!"

"Come on, Sam! There isn't any more time! Help us now!"

The voices continued, but Sam was able to blur them out, entering his own state of grace because he saw something on the cavern wall that sparked his memory. Crawling at a snail's pace along the cavern wall was one of those bulbous, blueberry bug creatures.

Sam instantly remembered that when he was a slave minion, he had made a final push to escape from the Watcher's lair before it was too late and all of his life force was sucked dry. He remembered looking out from the darkness and seeing Bramilda, the blue witch, slurp up one of those bugs. She was detestable in doing so, mopping up the juices off her face. It was this memory that came to Sam, and this memory that saved the three friends from the evil witches.

Sam looked at the Emmys and Jacks, who had stopped twirling. The pleading had silenced. Sam walked over to the wall, pulled at the bulbous slug thing, which was quite large, roughly five inches in length. It took him a few pulls to break the suction the insect had on the wall, but finally it broke free to a popping sound. The insect left a slop of blue on the wall.

"Anybody hungry?" Sam said.

There was no real response from the Emmys and Jacks looking back at him, but he thought for a second one smirked. Whether it was approval of his plan, or because they were salivating over the bug, he did not know.

Sam tossed the large slug bug a few feet away and watched as one Jack and one Emmy launched themselves at it. Neither of the witches even had a chance to scarf it up, though. Before their mouths could reach it, their heads collided, clinking into each other to a massive knocking sound.

The witches were clearly and utterly knocked unconscious. Even more so, their potion had immediately stopped working. They instantly morphed back into their heinous forms.

Sam, Emmy, and Jack walked up and stood over the evil witch sisters.

"You did it," Jack said. "You really did it."

"You saved us," Emmy said.

"Aw, it was nothing. No sweat," Sam said, taking several steps away. "Let's get out of here."

Jack looked at Emmy, an expression of deep thought on his face. The previous events clearly were weighing him down.

"You okay, dingus?" Emmy said.

"Yeah, fine," Jack said. Jack thought about the kiss. It wasn't Emmy who he had kissed, but he so badly wanted it to have been. He had kissed Bramilda, the witch. *Ew.*

"Just glad everyone's okay," Jack said, walking ahead to catch up with Sam.

"Hey, dingus?" Emmy called out.

Jack turned around and was immediately caught by the wondrous green eyes of Emmy Wheatley, the real Emmy Wheatley. She was standing directly in front of him, merely inches away.

"Emmy?" The whole world stopped for Jack, his heart beating in rapid succession.

"Dingus?"

Wanting to stay trapped in that moment forever, Jack put his hand on Emmy's neck and kissed her. And it was magnificent.

Jack pulled his lips apart from Emmy's. This time, his lips came away with ease, and it was magical. He watched as Emmy slowly opened back up her green eyes, her hair beautiful chaos. An incredible smile formed on her face.

"So wait," Emmy said, still floating from the kiss. "Your first kiss was with Bramilda, the witch?"

"WHATEVER!" Jack said, turning around to catch up with Sam.

Emmy giggled to herself. Her giggle came to an abrupt halt, though, as she saw something out of the corner of her eye. Emmy walked up to Gramilda, who looked like she had been in a twelve-round fight with her sister. Her witch hat had fallen off, a huge lump was quickly forming, her tongue lolled out of her mouth, and her eyes were whites, the pupils rolling behind her eyelids. In a small satchel at the side of her waist, a small circular object hopped up and down in excitement.

Emmy opened the satchel and was reunited with Stony.

53

The Watcher looked in on his crystal-ball clock at yet another failure. He saw his evilest minions, the witch sisters, lying stone-cold knocked out on the floor. He wasn't upset. Not yet, at least. He had grown to understand the incompetence of all that surrounded him since those ratty children had entered the fold. He supposed it was inevitable that he would need to be the one to erase these children, to end them, to put the finishing touches on their little charade. They could march in unexpectedly and pull a fast one on him, they could outrun his monsters and they could outsmart the witches, but now it was his turn. The Watcher smiled, as he knew the children were close.

But then, he realized something that did, indeed, anger him. It made his blood boil and the veins on his temple throb in and out, up and down. Before the images on his crystal-ball clock faded away, the Watcher noticed that the small satchel he had given to Gramilda was gone. The children had again rescued their jagged, rocky little friend.

His anger only lasted a moment, though. The Watcher gained his composure, understanding the task that now lay ahead of him. It was no matter that they rescued Stony. After he ended the children and ruined their little field trip of destiny, he would crush the stone. This time, he wouldn't give him a chance to live; he would pound the stone to dust.

The Watcher, knowing what he needed to do, walked away from his crystal-ball clock and over to his clock tower. He looked out at the massive structure, the thing that held his power. He felt it coursing through him, and it hadn't been this strong in a long, long time.

The time had come. Feeling the power of the clock tower, fueled by the souls of all the children he kept as his slaves, the Watcher prepared himself to summon it all.

The pale children kept twisting, dialing, and turning, but the clock tower itself began pulsing with energy. The giant face of the clock that stood atop the tower turned from white to green and radiated energy.

The Watcher looked on in delight and prepared to use his mighty force on the three pesky best friends and their little stone sidekick.

54

Sam, Emmy, Jack, and Stony walked and rolled on. They followed the ticks and tocks of the clocks that were now all around them. Various clocks, all different sizes and shapes, surrounded them. Each belonging to a child, holding the remains of their soul. Whatever part the Watcher allowed them to keep.

"This is it," Sam noted. "I remember this cavern."

"Yeah, so do we," Emmy said, looking on past the clock walls and seeing the opening to the clearing where the clock tower resided.

Stony rolled back and forth, small motions. He wasn't entirely too keen on where they were at in their journey. He knew this part was inevitable, but he was scared, nonetheless.

"Are we ready to do this?" Sam said.

"We bested him once and escaped this place. This time, we finish him," Jack said, pulling back his slingshot and launching air.

"I don't mean to be the bearer of bad news here,

boys. But how exactly are we going to do this?" It struck Emmy just then that they didn't really have a plan. She just kind of assumed that they would figure it all out when they were down here. And she was exactly right. That's the way the three besties always did it, and that wasn't going to change.

"It's the clock tower," Sam said. "It holds all of his power. We destroy the clock tower, we destroy the Watcher, and we rescue the children."

"Maybe we can light the puppy on fire!" Emmy said.

Sam pulled out the lighter he had loaded in his pocket, and he looked down at it.

Emmy was making explosion noises and motions with her hands when a loud and long rumble exploded from the direction of the clock tower.

The three besties and their stone companion immediately turned their heads in the direction of the noise.

"He knows we're here," Sam said.

"Whatever happens, you guys are my best friends. Stony, you too, buddy," Jack said.

Emmy hugged her two best friends tight. Then she bent down to meet Stony at eye level. "You ready to do this, buddy?"

Stony hopped up once, indicating that yes, indeed he was ready.

They began a light jog over to the loud crackle-bang they heard. Emmy, a fairy with one working wing. Sam, a vampire count whose cape had fallen off somewhere back in the cave. Jack, muddled, filthy and Stony, ready to take on the challenge.

When they exited into the clearing where the clock tower stood, the feelings of emptiness came rushing back. It was as massive and hulking as ever. Bits of bright lightning crackled throughout its wooden pillars. The children stood throughout its many levels unfazed. They went on twisting and pulling, working.

The final countdown was on, and the friends knew that their time was near. If they were going to end this thing and save the day, they needed to act right then. The only problem was what their attention was fixed on next. Standing not far from the clock tower, draped in his massive muscles and scaly green armor, the Watcher stood with his arms high in the air. The lightning crackling all around the cavern, up and through the clock tower, emanated from the Watcher.

Sam wasted no time and sprinted toward the clock tower, evading a green lightning bolt that had shot down from the top of the clock tower. He lunged away, quickly gained his composure, and kept on running.

The Watcher stared at the feeble children; their attempts amused him. He continued to exude energy, pulling it from the clock tower and using it for his own advantage.

Another large pulse of green light shot down from the clock tower at the ground and opened up a crack in the dirt. From it, heinous monsters began rising up and out. Ghouls, hairy beasts, and pumpkins that hopped along the floor with razor teeth and other frightful things rapidly climbed out of the hole, as the lightning subsided and the Watcher rested his arms at his sides. He looked on in delight at his monsters.

Sam began beating away at the clock tower's base with his baseball bat. He realized quickly that wasn't going to work. The wood of the clock tower was too strong from magic. It wouldn't budge or crack in the slightest. There's no chance it would break.

A horrifying pumpkin hopped quickly along and leaped up at Sam, ready to sink its gnarly teeth into him. Sam turned his attention, lifted his bat, and swung for the fences, launching the pumpkin at the wall of the cave, its innards exploding everywhere.

Jack and Emmy stood back-to-back, looking out at the terrible things that were rapidly approaching.

"What do we do?" Emmy said.

Jack had his slingshot at the ready, prepared to use it. The only problem was he had no rocks, no ammunition. "Got any rocks?" Jack said nervously.

Stony jumped up and down, doing his best to signal Jack. *USE ME!!*

Jack looked down, saw Stony, and the idea came instantly. "Are you sure about this, dude?"

Stony hopped up once.

Glancing at a werewolf-looking beast that was creepily crawling over to him, liquid seeping down from its snaggle tooth, Jack picked up Stony, rearing him back in the slingshot and launching it at the werewolf. It was a direct hit between the eyes. The werewolf whimpered, cowering in pain, and it ran off into the shadows.

"All right, direct hit!" Jack said.

"Way to go, dingus!" Emmy then noticed a troll had come shuffling over to them, his mini ax in hand. The troll lifted it into the air. "Jack, watch out!"

Stony speedily rolled back to Jack.

"Not this time, booger brains." Jack picked up Stony again, launching him back and letting him rip from the slingshot directly between the eyes of the troll. The force of the shot knocked the troll off its feet, clearing him a few feet.

The troll lay stunned, motionless.

Sam pulled out the lighter from his pocket. "Here goes nothing," he whispered to himself, igniting the flame of the lighter and setting it to the clock tower. "Come on!" Sam yelled. The clock tower would not light. Sam looked up at the face of the clock tower, which must have been two hundred feet high in the air. Massive, it stared back at him with grinning eyes and an evil smile. "Come on, come on!" Sam yelled even louder, but no matter how loud he was, it did not matter. The clock tower would not light.

This time, Sam was not quick enough. Another pumpkin had hopped up from behind him and planted itself directly on Sam's head. Sam felt the squishy insides of it wrapping around his face. He clawed at it, doing his best to rip the thing off his face. Its pull was too tight, and he felt it squishing around his nose and his eyes, trying to completely attach itself, trying to make itself Sam's new face. Sam fell to his knees, still doing his best to tear the pumpkin off of his own head.

He looked on through the eye holes of the pumpkin at his two best friends, who were trying to fend off their own wave of monsters.

Jack kept launching Stony at various monsters that crept at them. One by one, he picked them off, but there were too many, and they kept rising out of the hole in the ground.

Jack took aim at a Frankenstein-looking thing that was slowly marching, step by step, over to where he and Emmy were standing. That was not the thing he had to worry about, though. Before he even had a chance to launch Stony at the Frankenstein thing, a translucent ghost—a real ghost—had scooped him up and was prancing around, dangling Jack several feet in the air. Jack dropped the slingshot and Stony to the ground as he was whisked away. A hand puppet for the ghost, who Jack swore he could hear giggling.

"Jack, NO!" Emmy shrieked. She looked on in sheer fright at Jack, dangling from the ghost's grip. Then she looked over at Sam, who was still grappling with the pumpkin that had attached itself to his face. Emmy started bawling, tears exploding from her everywhere. "Jack!" she cried out. "Sam!"

Emmy's whole world was crumbling. They were defeated. There was no hope left. Without her two best friends, she was doomed. Soon, they would become pale, soulless minions of the Watcher. They would look on in terror as the Watcher rose back to the surface, fulfilling his prophecy and taking back control of the world above.

Stony hopped up and down, trying to indicate to Emmy that there was still hope. Emmy might have lost confidence in herself, in her friends, but not Stony. His newfound best friends hadn't quit on him, and he sure as heck wouldn't quit on them now. Stony hopped up and down on the slingshot. *THE CLOCK TOWER!*

Emmy understood him. An unspoken connection. She wiped a massive *shlosh* of tears from her face and looked down at the slingshot. She grabbed him, picked up Stony, and stormed herself in a sprint over to the clock tower.

My work is complete! the Watcher thought. He took in his surroundings, brimming with all the power and confidence in the world. He looked at one of the boys, his face now a ragged jack-o'-lantern. The Watcher, devilishly evil, giggled. The other boy was hanging by his shirt collar by a doomed spirit, screaming for help. His minions were running around, leaving chaos in their wake.

The Watcher lifted his arms again with sheer dominance showcasing his massive frame. *Where is the pesky girl, though? No matter, she was probably eaten whole by a werewolf. Or chopped into pieces by a troll.*

"My time has come!" the Watcher roared. "Finally, I will return up above! The world is mine once again!"

Emmy looked up at the clock tower, then back down at Stony. *What's going to happen to you?* Emmy realized right then that launching Stony into the clock tower would probably kill him. *Will this set his soul free? Will he be trapped as a rock forever?*

She picked him up but paused. "I can't do this."

Stony nuzzled around in her palm. *It's okay. You can do this. Set me free. Set us all free. End his evil.*

Emmy wiped another bout of tears that had formed in her eyes. She set Stony into the slingshot and pulled it back.

The Watcher realized before it was too late what was happening. "FOOOOOLLLL!!!! NOOOOOOO!!!!"

Emmy let the slingshot go and off Stony went, a rocket launching up into Earth's atmosphere.

It was a bullseye. A shattering of glass, a crackling of lightning, and a massive flash of green light all birthed at once, immediately upon Stony smashing the clock tower's face. A loud rumbling was heard from the base of the clock tower, and children all over woke up from their stupor. They looked around at their surroundings, mostly confused.

Ghosts, ghouls, and monsters were evaporating into various colors of dust all around the cave. Emmy saw the pumpkin around Sam's head dissipate into orange vapor, and Jack fell to the ground as the ghost disappeared.

"Let's run!" Emmy called out to her friends. The rumble of the cave grew even louder, heavy vibrations that caused the ground below them to shift and seize. All stemming directly from the clock tower.

Emmy, Sam and Jack ran as fast as their lungs would allow.

"FASTER!" Sam yelled.

"SHOELACES!" Emmy shouted to her two friends.

"What!?" Jack called back.

"SHOELACES!!" Emmy yelled again, panting, making it even harder to hear her.

"I CAN'T HEAR YOU!"

"SHOELACES! YOU DINGUS!"

And the three friends raced back through the cave, following the trail of breadcrumb shoelaces they had left behind.

They ran and ran until, finally, they reached the mouth of the cave. The opening where the door to the tree of time was led them back out into the surface of Mill Falls. Before they exited, all three friends took a long look back at the cave.

In that moment, they heard two things. The first was a giant explosion, which must have been the clock tower. The whole thing crumbling to dust, all of the Watcher's power and work crashing down to its demise. The other thing they heard was the voice of the Watcher.

"YOU CANNOT DEFEAT ME! I'LL BE BACK, HA HA HA HA HA HA!"

And with that, Emmy, Sam, and Jack took several steps farther and out of the nightmare.

55

ONE WEEK LATER . . .

Sam, Emmy, and Jack all sat around the kitchen table at the Strong residence.

"All right you go!" Mrs. Strong said, flopping down a piping hot box of pizza on the table.

"Mmm, my favorite!" Jack said.

"I'm starved!" Sam replied.

"I'll have a piz-za that!" Emmy joked.

Jack and Emmy quickly lunged for the big slices in the box. They both grabbed at two slices attached to each other and pulled them apart, mangling Emmy's slice in the process. A large hunk of cheese had come off with Emmy's slice and merged itself to Jack's. A new species of pizza, with double the amount of cheese and deliciousness.

Emmy looked over at Jack. She scowled in disapproval.

Jack carefully picked the wad of cheese that had come off of Emmy's slice and delicately placed it back onto Emmy's. He took a massive bite of his own, smiled at her through a mouthful of pizza, and grabbed her hand under the table.

Emmy smiled back.

Sam looked over at the TV, where a news report had come on. Reports of missing children all over Mill Falls was the top story and had been for the last week. Clips of parents in costumes from the week before, talking about skeletons attacking them, pumpkins walking on giant green stalks, and trolls, et cetera. The same clips were shown on repeat. Sam had seen these many times. More importantly, they had lived it. Noticing his mom was on her cell phone, Sam said, "So what do you think happened?" to his friends.

Emmy and Jack stopped slurping down their pizza and looked up.

"I think they're still down there," Emmy said.

"We freed them, I'm sure of it," Jack replied. "We all saw their faces. The children were all woken up from the evil spell the Watcher had on them."

"And what about the Watcher?" Sam said.

56

Reduced to a small shell of his former self, the Watcher sat alone on a pile of dirt. No longer the hulking being he was previously, his throne of clocks destroyed, now a small pile of ashy gray dust. The Watcher's once gigantic frame of heaping muscles and scales, teeth like razor blades radiating with power, was now a miniscule toy that only stood two feet off the ground. The Watcher raised his arms to garner energy, to garner power from the children, the souls he had stolen and kept as his energy resources. He summoned as much power as he possibly could, but his arms rose into the air and fell. He thought he felt a small spark radiate, but no power came of it.

"This is not the end. DO YOU HEAR ME!?" the Watcher screeched out. His voice was no longer destructive, nor did it rattle anything. It was high-pitched and squeaky.

Stumbling over to him, Gramilda and Bramilda entered his chamber, sporting giant knobs on their heads, red bulbs that had grown considerably since they bopped into each other.

"Master, master," Gramilda hissed.

"Where are you, master!?" Bramilda said.

"I'm down here, you numbskulls!" the Watcher called as loud as he could, looking up at the silly witches.

"Maybe he left us, sister."

"He didn't leave us, you foolish witch. He's our master, forever!"

"He might have left us; he was so angry, sister!"

"He would never, don't dare doubt his power!"

"I'm just saying that . . ."

Gramilda and Bramilda got themselves in yet another sister quarrel, yapping away at each other's foolishness.

"YOU IMBECILES!!!" the Watcher called out again, interrupting the witches' tittering.

"Oh, MASTER!" the witches said in unison, noticing their true leader not far off in the distance.

"Oh, you poor thing!" Gramilda lifted the Watcher up, a mother cradling her newborn baby, only this baby looked like an evil prehistoric monster.

"It's okay, master, he he he," Gramilda said. "We'll get you right and good in a jiffy."

"MORTAL CHILDREN! I WILL GET MY REVENGE!!" the Watcher's voice trailed off in a super high-pitched echo, as the witch twins carried their master off into the cave of nightmares.

57

William Clark stretched out as far as his young teen limbs could. He was achy all over, his eyes adjusting from the longest of sleeps. He felt disheveled, but he felt good. He stood and took one step with his wobbly legs, then another. The motions were awkward, but his muscle memory came back to him rather quickly. He had spent over a century as a small rock. It wasn't until the three bravest of best friends came to his aid that the curse had been broken, and his soul returned to him.

So many thoughts were racing through his brain. *Are my parents alive? My friends? Where am I? Will I be able to return home? Was the Watcher defeated?* He knew he had been saved, but he was so disoriented. He looked around and, realizing that he was still in the cave of nightmares, panic rose in his throat.

"I must find Emmy, Sam, and Jack," he whispered to himself.

William took several steps, gathering in the surroundings of the cave, until he heard voices. Low, but voices nonetheless. He followed them.

William kept walking until the voices grew louder and the cave opened up into a giant clearing. There, he saw the massive pile of gray ash where the clock tower had been. Memories of being captured, of his friends, of the entire adventure came rushing back to him. It was quite a lot for him to handle, but the important thing was, he had hope. Hope that had been given to him by only the truest of friends.

William walked closer to the voices and saw gobs of children in packs. They were all gathered around one another, making sense of what had happened. They, too, were taking in the cave of nightmares and the memories of how indeed they found themselves down in that nightmare room.

Even though Emmy, Sam, and Jack had left the cave —of that he was sure—looking around at the children, William didn't feel alone. He felt part of a family for the first time in many, many years.

William looked at the packs of children and smiled.

58

"Such a bummer that we missed out on trick-or-treating this year," Jack said.

"I think I've had enough Halloween for one year," Emmy replied.

"Enough Halloween?" Sam questioned her. "No such thing!"

"Hey, Sam? Remember when you had that nasty pumpkin glued to your face? Do you remember when I saved you from being a Halloween monster *permanently*?"

"Ah, that was nothing," Sam said, giggling. "Jack and I had the whole thing under control."

"Yeah, *okay*!" Emmy clapped back. "This dingus was six feet in the air being dangled by a ghost! You had it under control, all right."

"We totally did!" Jack said. "Bros for life, right Sam?" Jack slapped hands with Sam.

"For life!"

Jack launched himself onto the couch.

Emmy gave both boys a look of disgust.

"Okay, Sam. How about we go back down there, and I can put that pumpkin head right back on you? Would you like that?" Emmy said.

"That—yeah, that's going to be a big nope from me," Sam said, noticing Emmy was still looking at him and inching closer. "Emmy? Don't you dare." Sam backed away. "Emmy? Emmy?"

Emmy clawed her hands together, ready to let them fly straight into tickle mode at Sam, who was backed against the wall, nowhere to turn to.

"Jack, help!" Sam yelled out, half laughing and half screaming for his life.

"No can do, Sammy boy," Jack said, grabbing the remote and clicking on the TV in the basement.

Emmy sat watching with her sleeping bag around her head, her two best friends on her sides. They were watching *Hocus Pocus*. A local channel was still running Halloween movies.

"No more witches, please," Jack said.

"I love this movie!" Emmy said. "It's always been one of my Halloween favorites. Sam?"

Sam didn't respond.

"Hey, Sam, you good?" Jack said, also looking over at Sam, who was zoned out, staring down at the ground.

"So what now?" Sam broke his stupor and spoke.

"What do you mean?" Emmy replied.

"We beat him, it's over," Jack said.

"We won the battle," Sam said. "But I can still feel him. It's faint and almost like it's not there. But sometimes it hits me like he's still around, lurking somewhere, deep down in that cave. Waiting for the right time to strike again. And what about the kids? Are they alive down there? Do they need our help?"

Emmy and Jack thought long and hard about these questions.

"I suppose I could be up for another adventure. Jack?" Emmy said, putting her hand in the middle of their semicircle.

"An adventure without me? Yeah, *right!*" Jack cried out, adding his hand on top of Emmy's.

Sam smiled, and the trio of hands was complete.

"Of course, if we go back down there, we're going to need some kind of cool name that shows we're heroes. We need to name our group something awesome, like the Ghostbusters," Emmy said.

"What about the Besties?" Jack said.

"*Lame*, dingus. We can do better than that."

"What about the Watchers?" Sam said.

And then it hit Emmy right in the face—the name came to her, and it was decided.

"No. We are the Time Watchers," Emmy said, smiling.

The three best friends turned back to their movie and enjoyed a nice, quiet evening at home with a large bowl of delicious, buttery popcorn.

Afterword

The Time Watchers, my second book, is done and done, over and out! Often lately, I've needed to pinch myself to make sure I'm not dreaming. I'm still left in awe daily that I get to see books with my name and my design in full form, fresh out of the package, on shelves, and most importantly in the hands of readers. Writing books has been my lifelong dream since I was just a little guy. In fact, in my elementary school yearbook, I wrote that "When I grow up, I want to be a writer." Well, mission accomplished! Go me!

When I published my first book *Don't Call at ALL*, I truly didn't know what to expect. There was so much to learn and so much uncertainty for me in regard to publishing, marketing and getting my name out there. I still have so much to learn. However, what I know now that I didn't know then is that the indie horror book community is the bee's knees. It is the best. The outpour of support for not just my first book *Don't Call at ALL*, but for me as an aspiring author in general, a dreamer, was truly special.

When the book was first published, the horror book community championed the fact that I was a debut author and gave me so much confidence in myself which I didn't always have. The community opened up to me and welcomed me with loving arms. They read my first book, shared it and posted about it all over social media. The next thing I knew, the book was being read by so many incredible people and authors who I looked up to and have nothing but the utmost respect for. Gone were any questions of self-doubt. The community embraced my first book and I with so much love and care, and for that I'm grateful.

When I set out to write my first book *Don't Call at ALL*, my goal was to write a Goosebumps throwback. If you follow me on social media, you know that I am an R.L. Stine mega fan. So much so, in fact, that I won a contest in 2014 with a short story I wrote called *They Came at Midnight*. The first prize of this contest was the privilege of being R.L Stine's special guest at the *Faceoff* book premier party which took place at the Grand Hyatt on 42nd street in New York City. This was truly a special and validating experience.

Anyway, back to *Don't Call at ALL*. So, my goal was to write a book that was similar to what I loved growing up—a modern day Goosebumps story filled with technology and all the fun pressures of cell phones and social media kids deal with today. I think I accomplished my goal when writing the book. However, what I didn't accomplish was developing my own voice. Yes, *Don't Call at ALL* was fresh and original (or so I've been told), but it was still more or less a Goosebumps book. I wanted my second book to be mine. I wanted it to be something not just fresh and original, but something I could truly call my own. I think that I accomplished that with *The Time Watchers*.

I have so many people to thank for helping me accomplish my dreams of writing children's horror books. Near the top of this list is Dustin Holden. You might know him on social media as Dustin Can Read. Dustin has become a good friend of mine, and more importantly he brought me onto his podcast before I had done anything in the book community. This probably doesn't mean a whole lot to most, but for me it instilled a confidence that allowed me a voice to talk about the things I love—spooky books. Before I met Dustin, I was very unsure of myself and my writing. Thanks for having the bookish voice of an angel, Dustin, and—more importantly—for being a great friend.

Of course, where would I be without the amazing Cameron Chaney, who you probably know from his world-famous YouTube channel *Library Macabre*. Or maybe you know him because he is the author of the sensational books *Autumncrow* and *Autumncrow High*. Or perhaps for writing the most excellent foreword for the very book you just read! From the beginning, Cameron was a guy that I looked up to as a mentor. For whatever reason, he had reached out to me after reading an advanced copy of *Don't Call at ALL* and asked if he could do the interior work on it before it was published. He said he really enjoyed the book and wanted to help out in any way that he could. There were several authors that had done the same for his first book, and so he wanted to do the same for me. This was seriously a dream come true. I mentioned above how authors I truly looked up to had begun reading my first book. Cameron Chaney is number one on this list. The interior of *Don't Call at ALL* turned into connecting over horror movies which turned into podcasting together, and on it went. Now, while he did the interior for my second book *The Time Watchers*, I also had the privilege of having him on this project to do the foreword. Cameron, your love of books and all things spooky is contagious, thank you for the endless inspiration and all you've done!

Lastly, how can I possibly give proper thanks without acknowledging the uber talented and endlessly giving Nichi Arcane, AKA Dark Between Pages. If you aren't familiar with Nichi's social media accounts, do yourself a favor and familiarize yourself with her. She is a freight train of bookish excellence whose unwavering devotion to support indie authors and books hits like a wrecking ball day in and day out. She is relentless in her pursuit of boosting all of us in this community, for the sole reason that she loves all of us, she loves books, and she loves when indie authors are shown love and appreciation. Nichi, you have become the most wonderful bookie friend, and I truly know in my heart of hearts you are destined for greatness in this business (something you've already achieved in my book).

There are many people that mean a great deal to me, so here are some quick hit shout outs. I adore all of the following people or accounts, and they've all been a huge part of this book and my writing career: CS James of *Twisted Books to Leave You Shook,* Culliver Crantz of *Frightvision*, Quinnbook, Elizabeth Sagewood (your review of *Don't Call at ALL* made my life), Cameron Roubique, Alex (AKA Finding Montauk), Josh Marsella, L.J. Dougherty, Kelly Hooked on Books, Lorien Lawrence, Daniel of Iron Rain of Books, Maude Campbell, David Sodergren, Emily Terry and, of course, my sensational cover artist Alan Dellascio. Alan's work is just out of this world and without him, this book would never have been accomplished.

Finally, major love to my close family and non-bookish friends. Mom, Dad and Maxi—you guys are the best! Love you all the most. Zenda and Kanter—this journey of life could not exist without you two. Thanks for being the best sucky boyfriends out there. Until next time, spooks!

- Robbie Myles, New York City, 2021

Printed in Great Britain
by Amazon